More **SPHDZ** from Jon Scieszka
and Shane Prigmore

SPHDZ Book #1!

SPHDZ Book #3!

Book #2!

SPHDZ

Book #2!

*h*eadz

by Jon
Scieszka

Illustrated
by Shane
Prigmore

Sugar-Free Goodness by
Casey Scieszka

High-Fiber Extras by
Steven Weinberg

Simon & Schuster Books for Young Readers

New York London Toronto Sydney SPHDZ

SIMON + SCHUSTER
BOOKS FOR YOUNG READERS
An imprint of Simon + Schuster
Children's Publishing Division
1230 Avenue of the Americas,
New York, New York 10020

This book is a work of fiction. Any references to historical events, real
people, or real locales are used fictitiously. Other names, characters, places,
and incidents are products of the author's imagination, and any resemblance
to actual events or locales or persons, living or dead, is entirely coincidental.

SIMON + SCHUSTER BOOKS FOR YOUNG READERS is a
trademark of Simon + Schuster, Inc. • For information
about special discounts for bulk purchases, please
contact Simon + Schuster Special Sales at 1-866-
506-1949 or business@simonandschuster.com.
• The Simon + Schuster Speakers Bureau can bring authors to
your live event. For more information or to book an event, contact
the Simon + Schuster Speakers Bureau at 1-866-248-3049
or visit our website at www.simonspeakers.com. • Book design by Dan
Potash • The text for this book is set in Joppa. • The illustrations for
this book are rendered digitally. • Manufactured in the United States of
America • 0813 OFF • First Simon + Schuster Books for Young Readers
paperback edition September 2011
    4 6 8 10 9 7 5 3
The Library of Congress has cataloged the hardcover edition as follows:
        Scieszka, Jon.
        SPHDZ book #2! / Jon
        Scieszka ; illustrated by Shane
        Prigmore. — 1st ed.
        p. cm. — (Spaceheadz)
        Summary: The campaign to save
        the earth from being turned off is
        going well, but Michael K. must enlist
        fellow fifth-graders Venus and TJ
        to help hide the SPHDZ from Agent
        Umber, especially when they become
        involved in a school play.
        ISBN 978-1-4169-7953-1 (hardcover : alk. paper)
        [1. Extraterrestrial beings—Fiction. 2. Theater—Fiction.
        3. Schools—Fiction. 4. Spies—Fiction. 5. Family life—New
York (State)—New York—Fiction. 6. Brooklyn (New York, N.Y.)—Fiction.]
I. Prigmore, Shane, ill. II. Title. III. Title: SPHDZ book number two!
PZ7.S41267Sod 2010   [Fic]—dc22   2010015846
ISBN 978-1-4169-7954-8 (pbk)
ISBN 978-1-4424-1295-8 (eBook)

Chapter 741!

FSMMNMMRP

ƒßµµ˜µµ®π

SPA©EHEADZ ATTA©K!

Chapter 1!!

Bπåç´´´åɔω åttåç°/

The two aliens attacked P.S. 858 before the first morning bell.

They waved their slimy purple tentacles. They blasted laser bolts into the air. And, weirdly enough, they waved large shopping bags decorated with orange pumpkins.

A whole pile of kindergartners ran screaming into school.

A couple first and second graders tried to hide behind the monkey bars.

It was chaos, panic, and more chaos.

Michael K. and most of the fifth

1

graders stood back in their usual corner of the playground. They were trapped. Caught between the metal chain-link fence on either side and the fearsome purple and orange aliens in front of them.

"We are going to die!" yelled Ryan.

"Every man for himself!" yelled Jose.

The aliens slimed closer, cutting off any escape.

That's when Michael K. saw the third little hamster-size alien poking his head out of one of the shopping bags. He suddenly knew exactly who these aliens were.

"Oh, no," said Michael K.

The little alien waved a tentacle at Michael K.

Classmate Venus saw the little wave to Michael K. Venus gave Michael K. a punch in the arm. "What the heck is going on? Do you know these aliens?"

"Well," said Michael K. "Not really. Kind of. Maybe?"

"What?" said Venus.

The aliens raised their laser blasters.

Michael K. shook his head in confusion.

How had this gone so terribly wrong? The Spaceheadz had been getting better at blending in lately. Maybe they still weren't completely good at acting like real people. And the sphdz.com website wasn't getting as many hits as they had hoped. . . .

But that was no reason to completely freak out and just go all alien-blaster-attack crazy on everybody.

This would completely blow their cover.

This would be sure to attract the Anti-Alien Agency, AAA for short.

This would be sure to get Earth turned off.

There was no way Michael K. was going to be able to fix this mess.

The first bell rang.

Mrs. Halley appeared in the back door. "What in the world?"

The alien with the funny hair turned toward Mrs. Halley.

Michael K. covered his eyes.

Michael K. knew that life on planet Earth might soon be over.

He just didn't want to see it end this way.

Chapter 2

BAAAAAWK!

∫åååååΣ°/

T he giant chicken stood by the side of Fourth Avenue. He swung a large red cardboard arrow so that it pointed to the new restaurant.

Sergeant Sanders's Alabama Fried Chicken.

It wasn't really a demotion, Agent Umber felt. It was just continuing his usual AAA agent duties. Under cover. Under very deep cover.

Umber swung the red arrow. He gave a few chicken-head nods. Just to give the full chicken effect.

"Baawk, baawk!" screeched someone driving by.

So the chief had reassigned him. Said he was saving Umber for "something special."

Not a big deal. It just paid less than a full agent position. And the hours were a lot less than a full agent position. So Umber had found the chicken job on his own. So Umber was working a bit of a side job.

But the bad news was that the official pizza parlor mistake had been posted for all the AAA agents to see on the antialienagency.com website.

And the report had officially been named the Pizza Problem.

And Agent Hot Magenta's comments on the "Agent Buzz" were way out of line.

Those pizza guys *could* totally have been aliens. They sure looked alien.

"Baawk, baawk!"

How had it ever come to this?

Protecting the world by standing on Fourth Avenue in a chicken suit.

It had all started for Umber back in 1933, before he was even born. It had started with flashing lights moving across the deep purple New Mexico night sky.

Agent Sienna, Umber's dad, back then a young man with a bright future in the Agency, saw the red and green flashing lights racing across the sky.

He said the lights were moving too fast to be a jet. He said the lights turned into a large, saucer-shaped object. He said the saucer hovered over him and gave off a low hum like a thousand tuning forks. He said bright white lightning surrounded him and froze him. He said he was lifted into the air and sucked into the saucer. He said he was turned into a giant doughnut.

Agent Sienna could only remember getting dunked, then turning human again.

His AAA Time Clock showed that he was missing from his New Mexico watch post for seven hours. So

Agent Sienna was "relieved of active duty" by the first AAA chief.

Fired. Disgraced.

They said no one had ever been turned into an alien doughnut.

They said he must have just left his post.

When Agent Umber was little, he had always wondered why his dad was so jumpy around flashing lights, and Frisbees, and doughnuts. Then Umber read the Sienna Coffee Break File. Then he knew why.

And that's why he had worked so hard to become Agent Umber, of the AAA—to clear his family name.

And now he might never get that chance.

But he was still an AAA agent.

And so he would still protect and serve and always look . . .

"Baaawk!" clucked another Fourth Avenue driver.

An empty Coke can sailed through the air and bounced off Umber's chicken head.

. . . up.

Camouflage

A surprising number of organisms use camouflage to fool other organisms.

The black and white stripes of a zebra look a lot like tall grass to color-blind lions (and all lions are color-blind).

The stick bug looks like:

The leafhopper looks like:

Chameleons, octopi, and cuttlefish can change color.

Here is a picture of a polar bear in a snowstorm:

"Now, just one minute," said Mrs. Halley.

But the aliens didn't give Mrs. Halley one minute. They reached their slimy alien tentacles toward her. They turned their blasters on her.

Venus punched Michael K.'s arm. "Do something!"

It was too late to do anything. The aliens raised their tentacles. The aliens aimed. The aliens yelled:

"Trick or treat!"

Michael K. peeked through his fingers covering his eyes. "What?"

The rest of the fifth graders and Mrs. Halley stood frozen in stunned silence.

"Give us all-new, superflavor treats," said one alien.

"Or we will give you *SmackDown* tricks," said the other alien in a familiar deep voice.

"Wee eeeek eeeek," added the hamster-size alien.

The aliens popped the heads off their costumes.

They weren't aliens. They were Bob and Jennifer.

"Eee EEEEK!"

And Major Fluffy.

Some of the fifth graders laughed. Most of the class gave Bob and Jennifer funny looks.

Michael K. was relieved and confused and annoyed all at once. How was he supposed to explain this? He hurried over to help Bob and Jennifer get out of their alien costumes.

"Very excellent dress-up to look like something else, yes?" said Bob.

"No," whispered Michael K. "Why would you dress up like aliens?"

"It's what Earth persons do for Halloween," Jennifer whispered back. "Remember you told us?"

"Yeah," said Michael K. "But Halloween is

next month. We only dress up in disguises that one day of the whole year. Not any old day."

Bob kicked off the rest of his costume. He pulled out his sparkly pink Disney princess notebook. "Aha," said Bob. "I will note: Halloween one day of whole year. But one question—what is a year?"

"Oh," said Mrs. Halley. "I see what the problem is. Michael K., you and your Bulgarian friends need to study the calendar."

Michael K. started to disagree, then decided, as usual, that it would be better just to nod and not have to answer even more questions.

The second morning bell rang. Everyone picked up their backpacks and books and filed into school.

Classmates Venus and TJ walked up to get a closer look at Bob and Jennifer and Major Fluffy's costumes.

"Halloween," said Bob. "Just one day."

"All right, Michael K.," said Venus. "What is really going on?"

Michael K. started to say "Nothing." But then he

made a split-second decision. He needed help. So he just blurted out the truth. "Bob and Jennifer and Major Fluffy are Spaceheadz from another planet. They need our help. If they don't sign up three point one four million and one kids to be Space-headz, the earth gets turned off."

"Oh, really," said Venus. She and TJ looked at Bob and Jennifer and Fluffy. "I know they are strange. But aliens? From another planet? No way. Where is the proof? Come on. I'm a scientist. I don't believe anything without proof."

Michael K. didn't know what to use for proof. Bob had told him that Spaceheadz were not allowed to change wave shapes like they had before. They could get in big trouble. And Space-headz didn't have a flying saucer or the real lasers people wanted to see. They just had a remote. To change their channels.

"I don't know how I can prove it," said Michael K.

But as it turned out, he didn't have to.

Because that morning the lunch that Big Joey had stolen from one of the second graders had blueberry yogurt in it.

"Hey, check this out," said Big Joey, the only other kid on the now-empty playground. "Yoo-Goo. All Blue."

Joey opened the yogurt. He stirred it with that little spoon that comes under the lid. "Blue goo." Joey loaded a spoonful of yogurt and bent it back to aim it at Michael K.

"Oh no," said Michael K. "You don't want to do that."

Michael K. didn't know everything about Spaceheadz, but he did know one very important fact.

When Spaceheadz got very mad or freaked out, strange electrical and magnetic things happened. And Spaceheadz got most freaked out by anything blue and blobby.

Joey smiled a mean smile.

He flipped a blue blob of yogurt at Michael K.

The blue blob fell short and landed with a plop on Jennifer's shoe.

Jennifer looked down. She saw the blue blob on her shoe.

The morning air crackled. It suddenly felt heavy and supercharged—like just before a giant thunderstorm.

Bob spotted the blue blob.

Fluffy spotted the blue blob.

Then, at 8:30 a.m., Venus and TJ got all the proof they needed . . . and more.

WHERE WERE YOU WHEN?

Σ´·'®´ Σ´'®´ Ұø¨ Σ´·´~¿

Chapter 4!

I. TWELVE GEESE
8:25 A.M.

Twelve geese floated in the Pond in the southeast corner of Central Park.

They paddled into the morning sunlight at the far edge.

First one, then all of the others, raised their wings, flapped, ran along the water, and flew off together.

Following magnetic currents invisible to human eyes, they flew south.

II. THE AD FACTORY NY
8:25 A.M.

Dad K. made it to his office early. He put his coffee cup down on his workbench/desk.

He opened the package of poster-size ads.

His new client would be here soon. Dad K. didn't know much about them. Just that they called themselves DarkWave X, they paid cash only, and there was absolutely nothing about them online or in company files. At all.

Like they were invisible.

III. HAIR TODAY/ZIA
8:25 A.M.

Mom K. walked up out of the subway entrance.

She glanced at a V of twelve geese flying overhead.

She checked her watch and walked three blocks due west.

Mom K. switched her briefcase to her left hand and with her right hand pushed open the glass door to the Hair Today Styling Salon.

20

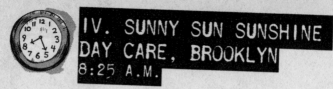

IV. SUNNY SUN SUNSHINE DAY CARE, BROOKLYN
8:25 A.M.

Baby K. sat in front of the TV.

The cartoon sun rose above the green hills.

The cartoon baby inside the cartoon sun laughed.

V. AAA HQ
8:25 A.M.

An orange and black butterfly flapped its wings once and landed on a square of cotton in the darkened room. Too dark to tell if it was a monarch or viceroy butterfly.

The AAA chief swiveled around in his giant black padded captain's chair. He stared at the butterfly.

"Quiet!" said the chief in a high, squeaky voice.

He swiveled back to face the curving wall covered in monitors showing maps and charts and graphs and multicolored shapes growing and shrinking, pulsing and spiking.

Joey pointed at the blue blob on Jennifer's shoe and laughed. He walked into school just as the 8:30 homeroom bell rang. All of the other kids and teachers were in the building, on their way to homeroom period.

So the only ones still on the playground, the only ones who actually saw what happened next, were:

1. Michael K.

2. Venus

3. TJ

And what happened next was:

1. Bob froze.

2. Jennifer's eyes opened very wide.

3. Fluffy's fur poufed out all over.

4. A wave of white and blue sparks flashed all over the chain-link fence.

5. The monkey bars wiggled and bent and jumped like they were alive.

Michael K. felt like a giant compass inside him switched everything from north to south and back again.

The three streetlights nearest the playground popped. Four car alarms honked and wailed. Two dogs across the street howled.

The monkey bars popped out of the ground, then suddenly collapsed into a tight ball of bent metal.

The chain-link fence jumped out of the ground, folded in on itself, and wrapped around the monkey-bar ball like a giant mesh doughnut, all the while still crackling and humming with a net of electromagnetic frizz.

The sparks and the hum grew larger and louder.

Jennifer's eyes opened wider and wider.

Bob twitched.

Fluffy vibrated.

The dogs howled. The school bell rang.

A line of sparks jumped from Jennifer, Bob, and Fluffy to the round ball of

monkey-bar metal. The instant the sparks touched the metal ball, a giant bolt of blue-white lightning flashed straight up into the sky.

A huge *BZZZZZZZRT* zapped the morning air.

Venus, TJ, and Michael K. felt a deep, invisible

pulse (like the lowest and loudest note ever) rumble

right through them.

All of the playground lights blazed on, then shorted out. Telephone wires sizzled. A small flock of four pigeons and six crows flew in mad, squawking circles in the sky. Two squirrels flipped somersaults on the basketball court.

Michael K. dived and wiped the blue blob off Jennifer's shoe.

"NOOOOO!!"

Fluffy's fur collapsed.

Bob let out a deep sigh.

Jennifer said, "Oops."

The sparks on the twitching fence and monkey bars died out.

The car alarms kept honking and beeping and bomping.

The 8:30 homeroom bell rang and rang and rang and rang.

Venus and TJ stared at the mangled doughnut pile of chain-link fence and playground equipment.

Venus and TJ looked back at Jennifer and Bob and Michael K.

"Okay," said Venus. "That's pretty convincing proof. But I would still like to hear a scientific explanation."

Well," said Jennifer.

"Because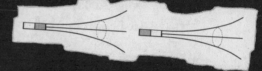

the

and then !"

"Okay," said Venus. "I got absolutely none of that."

"Eeee eee weee," said Bob's Tinker Bell lunch box. Fluffy poked his head out.

"Yes," said Bob. "Everyone knows that. You always think you have a better plan."

"Eeee EEE eeek EEEK!" said Fluffy.

"Okay, fine," said Bob. "You explain it to Venus and TJ."

Venus looked at Major Fluffy.

E eek week," said Major Fluffy. "Eeek ee—"
Michael K. grabbed Major Fluffy and
quickly stuffed him into his coat pocket.

"Oh, no," said Michael K. "I don't think
Venus and TJ are quite ready for that."

"Mrreef eeeef," said Michael K.'s pocket.
"Mmeee reef fff sssss rrrr mmmmmm ph ffffff.
Eee rrrr rrrrhhhh ghghghgh—"

The 8:30 homeroom bell suddenly stopped
ringing. And the reason it had stopped ringing was because a large lady in a white school
nurse uniform had just smacked the bell with a
large wooden paddle.

Nurse Dominique spotted the fifth graders.

"Just because there is a little electrical problem does not mean that we do not keep to our schedule, children. You have five more minutes of homeroom. Let's get moving. I've got my eye on you."

Nurse D. smacked the palm of her hand with her paddle.

Michael K., Venus, TJ, Bob, and Jennifer hustled into school and up the old metal stairs.

Nurse D. followed them upstairs without seeing the twisted mess of metal on the playground.

Yikes, thought Michael K. *That was close.* They were so lucky that Nurse Dominique had missed the Spaceheadz' whole blue-blob electromagnetic freak-out.

And so, so lucky that no one else had noticed either.

In her purple-lit Home Office Control Room, Agent
Hot Magenta spotted something suspicious on
her AAA NYC monitors. She traced a Con Ed

electric surge. She watched her magnetic compass spin wildly. She recorded a burst of crazy electronic Rice Krispies noise on the satellite feed.

Could be a solar flare. Could be something more.

Flocks of pigeons twisting like a tornado over the Brooklyn Bridge. Air traffic control at all the airports going nuts. Three dogs howling outside her window.

Wow!

Magenta replayed everything twice to be sure.

No doubt about it. This was a massive Alien Energy Wave.

And it was at D-7.

Wasn't that the same hot spot from just a month or two earlier?

Wasn't that the case handled by Agent Umber?

She would deliver this news directly to the chief.

She wouldn't bumble this like Agent Umber had last time. She would show everyone how to run this by the AAA book.

Agent Magenta flipped open her cool-looking SpaceshipPhone®. She speed-dialed 1.

"Three blind mice. Three blind mice. Sir."

Magenta listened to the chief's coded reply.

"Massive AEW at D-7, sir," said Agent Magenta. "Electric, magnetic, and biological signature confirmation."

Pause.

"You're welcome, sir. I am ready to move out right now."

Pause.

"Really, sir? I just thought—"

Pause.

"—and to always look up . . . sir."

Magenta plopped down into her AAA chair.

Magenta clicked her SpaceshipPhone® shut. This was not fair. Why couldn't the chief put her on this case? This was huge! And what agent could he possibly have on the case already?

1. TWELVE GEESE
8:30 A.M.

At exactly 8:30 a.m., something wrinkled the earth's magnetic field. The usually strong and steady flow north and south went east and west, and then shorted out.

Twelve geese flying south over New York City suddenly had no magnetic path to follow.

The geese took a sharp right turn. They took a left turn. Flapping and honking, they zigged and zagged and spiraled over Brooklyn.

The twelve geese landed in Greenwood Cemetery.

And they wouldn't leave.

Dad K. leaned back on his metal stool to study the old ads that his new client was working from.

The ads were propped up on his workbench/desk.

The Ad Factory NY offices were in a plain glass and steel building. But the company had brought in bricks and rusted machines and old equipment to make the Ad Factory NY look like a real working factory.

"So, what is this new program? You need a new slogan. A jingle?" Dad K. asked.

The man in the dark blue suit and black sunglasses slid a black folder marked with a single red X across Dad K.'s desk. "We need more."

Dad K. opened the black folder . . . and actually whistled in surprise.

"You are holding the very latest in brain research," said the man in the suit, brushing factory dust from his pant leg. "We have pinpointed the spots in the brain that make decisions. Now we need you to come up with the words that can activate those spots."

"Wow," said Dad K. "That is big. That is huge. But who are you? What is this for? What are you trying to sell?"

Without removing his sunglasses, the man in the suit looked deep into Dad K.'s eyes.

"You don't need to know the answers to any of those questions. All you need to know is that you are working for DarkWave X and that you are not telling anyone about it. ANYONE."

The Ad Factory NY clock clicked to 8:30.

Dad K.'s fluorescent factory lights flickered. His "This Is a Refrigerator Magnet" refrigerator magnet fell off the metal file locker. His computer screen (built into an old drill press) went dark, then popped on again.

Dad K. and the man in the suit jumped to their feet. The DarkWave X guy checked the screen on his phone . . . then hustled out of the Ad Factory NY.

Dad K. called after him, "When do you need this? How long should it be? Should it rhyme . . . ?"

III. HAIR TODAY/ZIA
8:28 A.M.

"Hello, Chrissy. Good morning, Carol," Mom K. called to the Hair Today stylists at the shampooing sink and the hair dryers.

Chrissy nodded.

Carol nodded.

Mom K. sat in the last chair, near the back wall.

Chrissy pressed a small green button on her spray nozzle.

The back wall and last chair turned on a hidden post. The other side of the revolving wall clicked into place, looking exactly the same, with an empty chair.

Now on the other side of the wall, Mom K. stepped out of the beauty salon chair . . . and into the secret offices of her new job in New York, her newly created government organization—the Company.

The ZIA.

Mom K. walked down the gray-tiled hall-way. And just as she walked past the gray coffee-break kitchen, the gray metal micro-wave beeped. It flashed a lime green display of flashing symbols,

•...£ ⁰

like an alphabet from another world.

The microwave door popped open.

A car alarm just outside went off with a whoooop.

This caused Mom K. to look out the small side window.

So she never saw the lime green symbols switch to letters. She never saw the letters spell out a very interesting microwave-display-pad message.

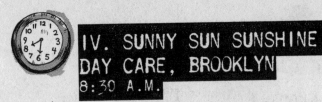

IV. SUNNY SUN SUNSHINE DAY CARE, BROOKLYN
8:30 A.M.

The cartoon baby inside the cartoon sun laughed.

The cartoon sun suddenly beamed its rays out in all directions.

The Sunny Sun Sunshine Day Care TV buzzed and went wavy for three seconds.

"Gooo," said Baby K. "Goo gaaaaaaaah."

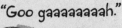

V. AAA HQ
8:35 A.M.

The chief had felt something deep and something large. He listened to the alarms just outside AAA HQ. He studied the pulsing monitors.

A small silver phone shaped like an ant . . . or maybe a spider . . . gave a very quiet insect buzz. The chief picked up the phone and listened.

"See how they run," he answered.

Pause.

"Yes, I see it, Agent Magenta. Good work. Thank you for bringing it to my attention."

Pause.

"I need you to stay put. Keep monitoring the situation. I have an agent on the case already."

Pause.

"You're not paid to think, Agent Magenta. You are paid to protect and to serve—"

Pause.

"Exactly," said the chief.

The chief killed the call. He dialed another with the punch of a button. He spoke into the phone: "Sat on a wall."

The chief listened. He spoke again in that high-pitched voice of his:

"Agent Umber, this is a Top Level matter."

Camouflage II

Organisms who might be prey use camouflage to hide.

But predators also use camouflage to disguise their attack.

Soldiers and hunters and spies use camouflage too.

Umber slapped at his Picklephone®, hidden in his pocket under his chicken suit. For some reason it had been going off like crazy—buzzing and twitching and playing ringtones Umber had never heard before.

It was probably the same electrical surge that had blown out the top of the Alabama Fried Chicken sign just a few minutes ago.

Rzzzz, rzzzz. Now the Picklephone® was buzzing again.

He kept it hidden, and on vibrate, because Sergeant Sanders was very picky about his chickens acting like real chickens.

You could get fired for Unchickenlike Activity While on Chicken Duty for something like talking on a phone.

Rzzzz, rzzzz. The phone buzzed once more.

This had to be a real call. And it had to be the chief. No one else had this number.

Umber ducked behind a skinny street tree and a garbage can.

He flopped around with his chicken wing and pulled out his phone. He opened it and heard a squeaky voice say, "Sat on a wall."

Umber replied, "Had a great fall."

"Agent Umber," said the chief, "this is a Top Level matter."

"Baawk—I mean, yes sir, Chief."

"Was that a chicken?"

"No sir, Chief." Umber flapped his wing to shoo away a small brown dog racing around in circles and snapping at his tail feathers.

"Sometimes the universe works in strange and powerful ways, Umber."

"Yes sir, Chief. Get off my tail!" Chicken Umber kicked at the dog.

"What did you say?"

"I said yes sir, Chief. I'm on the trail."

Silence on the Picklephone®.

"Agent Umber?"

"Yes sir."

"I have a plan for you. I mean—the universe has a plan for you. I can feel it. Can you feel it, Agent Umber?"

Now the dog was growling and pulling at Umber's tail feathers.

"Oh, yes sir, Chief. I can feel it, sir."

"Good. Because I know you and your family have had your issues with the Agency."

A fire truck thundered down Fourth Avenue, siren wailing, lights flashing.

"Yes we have, sir."

"But now it is time to protect and to serve. We have just recorded an enormous pulse in your territory."

"You mean that electrical surge—"

"That was no electrical surge, Umber. That was a massive AEW. And I need an agent on the case, right now. Agent Atomic Tangerine is stuck in traffic. Agent Screaming Green has a cold. You are our closest agent on the ground. This is your case, Umber. Get to D-7 as fast as you can."

The little dog yanked two of the long yellow chicken tail feathers free and ran around in circles.

Umber jumped to attention and saluted. "Yes sir!"

Sergeant Sanders picked that exact moment to step outside of his Alabama Fried Chicken shop. "What are you doing on the phone, Chicken? For Unchickenlike

Activity While on Chicken Duty—you are fired!"

"I quit," said Chicken Umber.

He took off his chicken head and handed it to Sergeant Sanders.

"You what?" said the chief.

"I said I never quit!" said Umber.

"Woof, woof," said the little brown dog, now spinning in crazy circles.

And he barked and spun up the block, following the running, man-headed chicken all the way up to Sixth Avenue.

Camouflage III

Not very good camouflage:

HoMEROOM

Chapter 11!

·øµ´®øøµ

8:45 A.M.

In the back of room 501-B Venus whispered, "This is the coolest thing ever!"

TJ nodded, doodling a sketch of aliens.

"Real aliens? Really from a different planet?" Venus bopped the back of Michael K.'s head with her pencil. "Why didn't you tell me sooner? This is crazy cool!"

Jennifer took the pencil off Michael K.'s desk.

Bob carefully added another unicorn sticker to his notebook.

Major Fluffy hopped on his wheel.

Michael K. tried to grab his pencil from Jennifer and half turned to whisper to Venus, "I've been trying to, but—"

"What planet are they from? How do they travel? Why do they need to collect brain waves? I've got a million questions!"

"They are Spaceheadz," Michael K. whispered.

Jennifer crunched the end of his pencil. Michael K. made a grab to get his pencil back. "And—"

"Michael K.," said Mrs. Halley. "I need your full attention up here. Why are you distracting your neighbors?"

Michael K. started to explain, "It's my only pencil. And—"

"And that is quite enough," said Mrs. Halley. "We have had so many interruptions this morning. There seems to have been some kind of power problem in different parts of the city. But the Board of Education has assured us that everything is fine now. So we must get back on schedule. And we do not have time for foolishness, do we, Michael K.?"

Jennifer finished Michael K.'s pencil.

Venus folded her hands and looked innocently straight ahead.

"No, ma'am," said Michael K.

"Precisely," said Mrs. Halley. "Now, as I was saying—today each group leader will pick the Big Buddies project for their group."

Michael K. started to space out and worry about how he was going to explain everything to Venus and TJ, whether that crazy AAA agent was still tracking them, and where he was going to get another pencil . . . when the voice of Mrs. Halley woke him up again.

"And since I have your attention, Michael K., why don't you pick first for your Big Buddies group of Venus, TJ, Bob, and Jennifer."

"Huh? What?" said Michael K. He squinted up at the titles on the board. He had no idea what any of these projects were. He scanned the list as fast as he could . . .

1. Fourth-Grade Math Quest

2. Story Editing with Third Grade

3. Second-Grade Social Studies All-Stars

4. Kindergarten Play

. . . and quickly picked the one that sounded the easiest.

"We'll take Kindergarten Play," said Michael K.

TJ frowned.

Venus gave Michael K. an annoyed look.

"We just have to play with kindergartners," said Michael K. "How bad could that be?"

Chapter 12

KINDERGARTEN PLAY
°^~∂´®©å®†´˜ ⊓˥åɎ

A little blonde girl named Madison smashed green Play-Doh into Michael K.'s hair.

"I can't do this puzzle!" a little guy in a red shirt whined at Venus. "You do it for me! Right now!"

The kindergartner sitting next to TJ swung his feet, kicking TJ's chair. "A killer whale weighs as much as a school bus. A killer whale has fifty teeth. A killer whale could kill you."

Venus's and TJ's little brothers, Hugo and Willy, had Bob and Jennifer trapped in the dress-up corner.

"I'm four years old," said Willy. "How old are you?"

"We are three thousand five hundred years," said Bob.

Michael K. leaned over. "He's just kidding."

"You are a fireman," said Hugo, putting the fireman's hat on Bob.

"You are the bad guy," said Willy, putting the pirate shirt on Jennifer.

Bob and Jennifer smiled. They looked thrilled.

Venus and TJ did not.

"I'm not too thrilled with your Big Buddies choice," Venus said to group leader Michael K.

"Me either," said TJ.

Miss Singer, the kindergarten teacher, clapped her hands three times. The kindergartners stopped what they were doing and clapped their hands three times.

Miss Singer sang, "CLEAN UP, CLEAN UP, EVERYBODY CLEAN UP."

All the kindergartners sang, "CLEAN UP, CLEAN UP, EVERYBODY CLEAN UP."

Miss Singer sang, "CLEAN UP, CLEAN UP, EVERYONE DO YOUR SHARE."

The kindergartners sang, "CLEAN UP, CLEAN UP, EVERYONE DO YOUR SHARE." And then, like magic, they all started cleaning up.

Madison put all of the Play-Doh cans back into a plastic bin and put it on the shelf.

The little guy in the red shirt scooped the puzzle pieces into a box and put the box on the puzzle shelf.

Hugo and Willy hung up the fireman hat and the pirate shirt.

"How does she make them do that?" said Michael K.

"It must be mind control," said Venus. "They never listen to me or TJ like that."

"Circle time," said Miss Singer. All of the kindergartners sat in a circle, with their legs crossed and their hands in their laps, on the rug at the front of the classroom.

Michael K., Venus, TJ, Bob, and Jennifer stood next to the class rules on the blackboard.

"Kindergartners, these are our fifth-grade Big Buddies," said Miss Singer. "They are here today and tomorrow to help us with our play."

Bob raised his hand and started talking. "We love to play. It's whole-grain fresh!"

"Four-wheel-drive power!" said Jennifer, flexing both arms in a classic muscleman pose.

The kindergartners laughed.

Miss Singer quickly took control.

"We love your enthusiasm," said Miss Singer. "And now I think we know what parts in the play will be perfect for you." Miss Singer smiled.

Michael K. found himself smiling back. He wasn't sure why. And then Miss Singer's last sentence sank into his brain. Michael K. stopped smiling.

"Excuse me, Miss Singer. Did you say 'parts in the PLAY'?"

"Why, yes," said Miss Singer. "We have been reading so many fairy tales. We decided to put on a Fairy Tale Play at this Friday's parent-student-teacher meeting."

"Sugar-free!" cheered Jennifer. "What is a Friday parent-student-teacher meeting?"

"Nonstick!" said Bob. "What is a fairy tale?"

"Oh, no," said Michael K. "This is a terrible mistake. We are not supposed to dress up or be in a play. We are just supposed to hang out and . . . you know, play."

"Friday night," Venus said. "As in **TOMORROW NIGHT** Friday night?!"

"Yes," said Miss Singer. "Tomorrow night we

perform 'Little Red Riding Hood' for all of the moms and dads and teachers and students. So let's get started with our play practice!"

The circle of kindergartners clapped and cheered.

"Michael K.," said Venus. "Remember five minutes ago when I said I was not thrilled with you?"

"Yes," said Michael K.

"I changed my mind. Now I hate you."

And that is exactly when the giant monkey opened the door and jumped into the room.

Chapter 13

MONKEY SEE

μø~°´Ұ β´´

EXACTLY SEVENTEEN MINUTES EARLIER . . .

Umber kicked off the last leg of his chicken outfit and stuffed it in the back of his slightly rusted, very dented white van.

He hopped into the driver's seat, fired up the engine, and zoomed off to Save the World!!!!

Attack! Attack! GO, GO, GO! screamed the network of nearly every cell in Umber's brain.

No, wait a minute. That's what got you in trouble last time, flashed a small network of new brain cell connections. *That is what gets you in trouble every time. Don't just ATTACK! ATTACK! GO, GO, GO! Why don't you try and make a Real Plan this time?*

Umber stopped at a red light and thought about a Real Plan.

The light turned green. Umber stepped on the gas and headed toward D-7.

Here were the facts:

1. A large AEW had been recorded at location D-7.

2. The chief had assigned Agent Umber to investigate the D-7 AEW right away.

3. D-7 was the same location as the last AEW Umber had investigated.

4. That investigation had not turned out well—scary school nurse, kickball accident, ant farm nightmares, lost agent shoe, no aliens.

Umber pulled his van up to P.S. 858. No parking spaces around for blocks. As usual. So he had to park next to a fire hydrant. Again.

Umber scanned the empty playground. Something big, something out of this world, was going on here. But what? Umber used every bit of his AAA training to search for clues. He took in all of the details—popped streetlights, disconnected school bell, chain-link fence twisted into a metal ring around a tangle of crushed monkey bars. . . .

Hmmmm. The aliens must be twelve feet tall and as strong as the Incredible Hulk.

Look for large green men in school? Could that be right?

Agent Umber remembered AAA Agent Rule #3: "Gather more facts."

Umber turned on the van radio. Maybe there would be

some kind of clue in the news, weather, sports . . . or traffic.

"Con Ed officials are still unable to say what might have caused the strange electrical surge this morning. . . ."

Umber twisted the radio dial.

"Knocking out streetlights, setting off alarms, and zapping phone service . . ."

Another twist of the dial.

"Possibly a solar flare, a freak lightning strike . . ."

Twist.

"The entire city, with the center in Brooklyn, seems to have been—"

Umber punched the off button.

Hmmmm. Large green men with electric sparks shooting out of their eyes?

Agent Umber spotted two squirrels on the playground basketball court. They were sitting on their hind legs, facing each other. And it looked like they were playing patty-cake.

"Hmmm," said Umber. "Now, that has to be some kind of clue."

Outside P.S. 858 a class bell rang. And rang and rang and rang, then suddenly cut off. Like someone had unplugged it. Or maybe hit it with a large wooden paddle.

Whatever the aliens looked like, they had to be in there

somewhere. And as an AAA agent, Umber had sworn to protect and to serve, and to always look up. He couldn't just sit still. This was his chance to be a hero, to save the world, to finally clear his family name. He had to do Something. The world was counting on him. The chief was watching him. But what to do? What to do?

Umber banged his fist on the AAA van dashboard. The glove box popped open. A grease-stained book fell out. And there was Umber's answer—the AAA manual.

Umber picked up the AAA manual (secretly disguised to look like a White-Van repair manual). It was open to chapter 23, "Investigations."

Step 1. Use disguises. Be original. Look like something completely unexpected. Hide in plain sight.

Of course. That was it! Umber jumped out of his van, threw open the back doors, and dug through his collection of disguises-on-the-go. No one did disguises like Umber. The chief had told him that once. And he wasn't kidding.

Umber flipped through his fake moustache, his clown suit, and his Spider-Man, princess, plumber, and astronaut disguises. . . .

Not very original.

Pirate, ghost, Darth Vader, Dora the Explorer . . .

Not very unexpected.

And then Agent Umber saw the answer to his question.

It was original. It was unexpected. It would get Umber inside school without anyone knowing who he was. And it might just get him a free banana or two. Umber liked bananas.

Umber's brain flashed: *YES! YES! YES! GO! GO! GO!*

So Agent Umber put on his perfect disguise and headed into D-7, the Alien Hot Zone, P.S. 858, dressed as one very tall monkey.

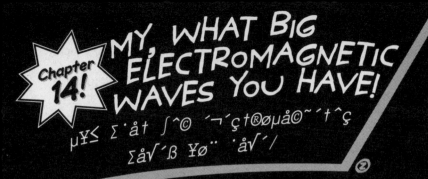
I am so sorry for that interruption, boys and girls," said Miss Singer. "Apparently, that man was selling bananas to the school cafeteria and lost his way. Thank you to our new fifth-grade Big Buddies for helping him down to the office."

Jennifer raised both arms overhead in a big-time wrestling victory pose.

The kindergartners clapped and cheered.

"Though maybe next time we can practice using our words. And not our fists and legs . . . and elbows."

"Okay," said Bob. "We were walking down the hall with the monkey, and then he started running, and you are not supposed to run in the halls. . . ."

"So I took him down with a flying scissors kick," said Jennifer. "And then popped him with a spinning headlock chop block."

"Well," said Miss Singer. "That's not exactly what I meant about using your words. But let's get started on our play practice. Who can explain our fairy tale story to our fifth-grade Buddies?"

Half of the kindergartners raised their hands. The other half started talking all at once.

"Remember we raise our hands?"

"And then go to the bathroom," added Bob.

"He said 'bathroom'!" said Hugo.

Willy and Hugo started laughing.

Before the circle got any more out of control, Miss Singer called on Jessica.

"The story has a wolf and he dresses up like my granny," said Jessica. "And then he tries to eat the little girl and then she says, 'My, what big eyes you have' and 'My, what big teeth you have,' and she wears a red coat and that's why they call her her name, Little Red Riding Hood, and we are all Red Riding Hoods so we can all be the stars of the play."

Bob grabbed Jennifer. "What?! The wolf dresses up like the granny and tries to eat the little girl? Why would he do that? That is not naturally sweetened! We have to stop this wolf."

The small electric pencil sharpener next to Bob went off without anyone touching it.

"**SPHDZ** will help the Red Riding Hoods be **RAM TOUGH**," said Jennifer.

A pile of metal paper clips on Miss Singer's desk bunched into a doughnut shape.

Now the circle of kindergartners officially went crazy, laughing and squirming and poking one another.

Michael K. whispered to Venus, "This is not good. That giant monkey we just chased? I'm pretty sure he is the AAA agent who almost caught us last time."

Venus raised an eyebrow. "That is definitely not good. And have I told you that I hate to do this kind of play stuff?" Venus held out her arms to show off her costume: Little Red Riding Hood's Mom. "It's just so . . . ugh."

TJ hefted his Friendly Woodsman cardboard ax. "And you are so lucky I am a *friendly* woodsman."

Miss Singer divided everyone into play practice groups. She got the whole mess of kindergartners to put on their red riding hoods.

Miss Singer chanted, "We are stars."

The red-cloaked kindergartners repeated, "We are stars!"

"We are stars," Miss Singer prompted.

"We are stars!"

"They don't look like stars," said Michael K. "They look more like a gang of garden gnomes."

Miss Singer handed the fifth-grade Buddies their scripts.

"I am Granny," said Jennifer in the deepest Granny voice ever.

"I am a Woodland Creature!" said Bob, thrilled to be putting on bunny ears.

Miss Singer herded the whole class of kindergarten

Red Riding Hood stars toward the block corner for the first scene at Red's mom's house.

"Okay, places everyone!"

Jennifer decided to try Miss Singer's chanting . . . with a slight change of her own.

"Granny rules," boomed Jennifer.

Hugo and Willy repeated, "Granny rules!"

"Granny rules."

"Granny rules!"

Bunny Bob crouched near the arts shelf, showing Little Red Jessica and Little Red Steven how to hop like a bunny. It was kindergarten chaos.

Michael K. didn't really want to add to it. And he was afraid he already knew the answer to the question he didn't really want to ask. But he had to ask.

"Um, Miss Singer?" said Michael K. "I have a whole script with all of the lines, and I don't have a costume. What's my role?"

Miss Singer quieted Jennifer and her gang, separated

Bob and his bunny followers, and waved a hand toward a big green file cabinet. "Bottom drawer."

Michael K. opened up the green cabinet and pulled out a large, gray, furry bundle. Michael K.'s bad feeling about his role was confirmed. Michael K. put on his wolf costume.

"So how are we going to collect millions of Space-headz, but still hide from this AAA guy?" said Venus.

Michael K. put on his very big head with very big eyes and very big teeth. "Good question," said Michael K. "I'm still working on it."

This was terrible. This was embarrassing. And he wasn't doing a very good job of saving the world.

Michael K. wondered if his life could get any worse.

It did.

Granny Jennifer took one look at Wolf Michael K. and said, "If you try to eat one of my Little Red Riding Hoods, I will atomic-butt-drop you."

And she meant it.

Mimicry

Camouflage is one way to hide.

Looking like something you are not is another great way to hide in plain sight. It's called mimicry.

The coral snake is very poisonous.

The king snake is very harmless.

But because the king snake mimics the look of the coral snake, no one bothers it.

The sweet-tasting viceroy butterfly manages to stay uneaten . . .

by mimicking the look of the nasty-tasting monarch butterfly.

MONKEY BUSINESS

Chapter 15!

μø~°´¥ ∫¨ß^~´ßß

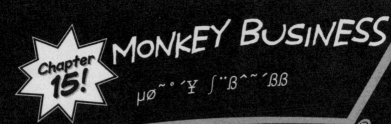

The tall monkey crouched inside the green plastic recycling bin in the corner of the cafeteria-gym-auditorium. He rubbed his sore shoulder. He felt the knot on his head. Not good. Where had that little kid learned a spinning headlock chop block? She really nailed it. Solid.

Okay. Maybe it hadn't been such a good plan to go with the monkey disguise. To just pop into every classroom and look for aliens.

Funny-looking bunch of kids in that last classroom. Some big. Some small. Maybe that's how they did it these days. Couple of them did look very familiar.

Well, whoever they were, Monkey Umber had given them the slip. Did the old turn-the-corner-and-hide-behind-the-door trick. They ran right past. Monkey Umber had jumped into this recycling bin. And now he had a foolproof plan. Wait here until school was over. Wait until everyone was gone.

Then Monkey Umber would have the run of the whole school.

Then Monkey Umber would track down the source of that AEW.

Then Monkey Umber would catch the aliens, save the world, and clear his family name for good. And Agent Hot Magenta might just see what a hero he was. She might even write a really long entry in the "Agent Buzz" about how great he was and how much she really liked him, and then she would—

BRRRRNG!

The sound of a wooden paddle hitting the fire bell snapped Umber out of his daydream.

BRRRRNG!

Another whack.

Somebody . . . or something . . . was messing with the fire alarm!

A clue! From chapter 3 of the AAA manual, "Alien Habits and Habitats":

> Aliens, and their Energy Waves, have been known to affect devices electrical or magnetic.

What a lucky break! The aliens hiding in P.S. 858 were right outside his bin!

Careful. Careful. Umber didn't want to scare them off. But he had to see what the aliens were disguising themselves to look like.

Umber rose up slowly from his crouch. He peeked out of a crack just under the green plastic bin cover.

He caught a glimpse of a blue New York Yankees jacket. A pair of white shoes.

The gym teacher!

The nurse!

Of course, thought Umber.

The gym teacher had been in the yard the day of that first AEW. And so had the nurse. And she was at the grocery store where the other AEW was reported. How could he not have figured it out sooner? Gym teacher and school nurse. Those were perfect disguises. Who would ever think they were aliens? They were always strange.

Umber dropped back down to the bottom of the recycling bin. He hid himself under the old handwriting workbooks and listened to the aliens' plans.

". . . crazy power surge . . . whole city . . . ," said the man's voice.

". . . we'll fix that . . . ," said the woman's voice.

BRRRRNG!

Another whack of wood paddle on metal fire bell.

Wow. This was it.

The aliens were planning to short out the whole city with a giant Alien Energy Wave . . . and no fire alarms!

Umber quietly pulled out his Picklephone® and sent a Level Red text to the chief:

SOURCE OF AEW FOUND.
BRINGING ALIENS IN NOW.

And just as Umber pressed Send, the bin cover flung open. A box of old fourth-grade MATH IS COOL! textbooks smashed into Umber, pinning him to the bottom of the bin. He couldn't move. Could barely breathe.

BOOM, BOOM, BOOM, CRASH, BOOM, CRASH, BOOM. More boxes piled on top.

Voices. Footsteps. The bin cover slammed shut.

"Roll it outside to the truck!"

Umber felt his bin moving.

His foolproof plan had been fooled again.

The last thing Umber heard in the gym was a short alarm bell ring, one voice saying "That fixes that," and then two voices laughing.

Mimicry II

Lots of birds and wasps like to eat spiders.

Nobody likes to eat ants.

So some sneaky spiders have evolved to mimic the look of ants.

These spiders even act like ants—they wave their two front legs in the air to look like ant antennae.

They walk with jerky, zigzag movements like ants.

Some of the spiders squirt scents to smell like ants.

Even the ants think they are ants.

Venus, TJ, Michael K., Bob, and Jennifer walked down the sidewalk kicking the piles of fall leaves. Bob stopped to pet a fire hydrant, then slapped a BE SPHDZ sticker on it.

Jennifer picked up a beautiful orange oak leaf, twirled it around to check both sides, and then popped it in her mouth.

Major Fluffy poked his head out of Bob's backpack.

"Eeee eek eeek?" asked Fluffy.

"Yes," answered Bob. "You missed the whole Red Riding Hood play. But I'm sure that your 'Fluffy for President' PowerPoint presentation is very good. And you should not worry about Speedy the class turtle."

"This has got to be the strangest day of my whole life," said Venus.

"It's like the craziest comic ever," said TJ. "Except we ar[e] right in the middle of it happening."

"Welcome to my world," said Michael K.

"So, we need more Spaceheadz," said Venus.

"Right," said Michael K.

"Or Earth gets turned off."

"Right."

"What does that mean?"

"I have no idea," said Michael K.

"Boy, you are a lame scientist. And a worse detective," said Venus.

Bob suddenly froze and held up one hand: "Don't walk!"

"What?" said Venus.

Bob, still frozen, tilted his head toward the crosswalk sign.

Everyone waited at the curb for the light to change.

TJ pointed to a line of ants spiraling up the light post. "Look at these crazy guys. You ever seen ants doing that?"

"What's so weird about that?" said Michael K.

"Ants don't usually do that," said TJ, holding one black ant on his fingertip.

"How do you know?" asked Michael K.

"TJ is an expert," said Venus. "He knows everything about bugs."

"Insects," said TJ, putting the ant back with his other ant buddies.

"Walk!" called Bob.

"So what are you doing to sign up Spaceheadz?" Venus asked Michael K. "How many do we have?"

Michael K. rolled out his skateboard and rode it across the street. "Well, we made a sphdz.com website. And we've got a couple thousand people signed up so far."

"A couple thousand?" said Venus. "That's it? That is nowhere near three point one four million and one."

Michael K. kick-flipped up the curb. "I've been busy!

I've got homework to do. I've got parents to deal with."

Bob picked a one-legged Barbie doll out of a trash can and slapped another BE SPHDZ sticker on the side of the can.

Something buzzed in Jennifer's backpack. She pulled out an electronic talking Spider-Man action figure. She held it up to her ear.

The Spider-Man figure beeped a series of tones.

Jennifer nodded.

Jennifer beeped three tones back.

She put Spider-Man back into her bag.

"General Accounting," said Jennifer.

"What does that mean?" said Venus.

"I forgot to tell you," said Michael K. "He's the Spaceheadz back at their planet that we have to report to. Come on, hurry. We have to get to Jennifer's command post."

"What is that?"

"You'll see," said Michael K.

Venus saw.

Venus stepped through the Spaceheadz door and saw probably the strangest thing she had ever seen . . . or at least the strangest thing since Jennifer's monkey-bar-crumpling freak-out that morning.

Inside, the Spaceheadz' house didn't really look like a house. There were no couches, no beds, no rugs, no regular house stuff. It was just one big room, crammed with all kinds of . . . stuff.

TV screens, radios, clocks, computer parts, kitchen appliances, vacuum cleaners, WWE wrestling posters, remote-control toys, lamps and neon lights, action figures, the old club jukebox, and lots of models of jet fighters covered the back wall.

Bob put his backpack down in a corner completely wallpapered with posters of the cutest kittens, puppies, horses, bunnies, unicorns, and fire hydrants. Bob added his newest find to an army of My Little Ponies, Polly Pocket dolls, and Disney princesses covering a table.

Fluffy hopped out of the Tinker Bell lunch box inside Bob's Dora backpack and ran over to a tangle of colored plastic hamster tubes surrounded by the smallest TVs ever, the portraits of every U.S. president, and a crazy collection of campaign posters and buttons and bumper stickers.

Boxes and bags, cans and bottles, tubes and packages of random products were everywhere. Toilet paper, cereal, laundry detergent, toothpaste, shampoo, old shoes, new garden hoses. . . . Every bit of free wall space was papered with newspaper flyers, ads, and signs.

TJ took it all in and said one word that pretty much described it all: "Whoa!"

Jennifer sat down in front of a microwave packed into the middle of the back wall. She cranked an eggbeater that was attached to a George Foreman grill with a GI Joe action figure wired to it. Everything on the wall lit up.

Jennifer's microwave hummed and then beeped. The GI Joe spoke the words that appeared in green letters on the microwave screen:

SPHDZ REPORT. SEND NUMBERS NOW.

Jennifer waved one hand, and sphdz.com appeared on the biggest TV screen in the pile.

The sphdz.com counter showed 7,351. Jennifer raised GI Joe's arm. The number 7,351 appeared in the microwave, flashed, and disappeared.

"What the heck is going on?" said Venus.

"Jennifer is reporting to General Accounting," said Michael K.

Venus looked up at sphdz.com. "And that's it? Your website?"

"Yeah," said Michael K.

"Well . . . ," said Venus, searching for something nice to say. "It's a good start. I can definitely add some design zip."

"It's got to look sharp," said TJ. "Otherwise nobody will want to join up."

The microwave hummed and beeped again. GI Joe delivered General Accounting's bad news:

VERY SLOPPY WORK.
YOUR E-WAVE COULD HAVE CAUSED
A CLASS THREE MESS.
AND YOU MAY HAVE ATTRACTED THE AAA.
NOT GOOD.

"Oh, man," said Michael K. "How far did that playground freak-out go?"

GI Joe continued General Accounting's message:

YOU HAVE ONE HOUR TO SPHDZ ONE MILLION HUMANS. FROZEN DINNER. DEFROST. POWER OFF.

The microwave powered off and went blank.

"One hour?!" yelled Venus. "Are you kidding me? Call that general back. Tell him we are working on it. Tell him we need more time!"

Bob and Jennifer smiled.

Bob held up a box of SuperCrunchies. "We are not worried. Michael K. can do anything."

Michael K. did not feel like he could do anything. He felt like he was going to throw up.

There was no way to sign up one million Spaceheadz in one hour. It looked like fifth grade was as far as he, or anyone in this room, was going to get. Earth was doomed.

0:01

Venus held the box of SuperCrunchies and looked at the picture of Michael K. in his super-hero outfit.

This only made Michael K. feel worse about the end of the world.

TJ held his breath, and looked as bad as Michael K. felt.

"Well, I'm glad you and Jennifer are not worried," said Venus. She checked the time on her pink rhinestone phone. "Because now you have exactly fifty-nine minutes to sign up one million Space-headz. I'd say we are toast."

Bob looked at Venus's phone. "Oh, no. **WE TRY HARDER**," said Bob. "Not one hour of Earth minutes. We have one hour of [SPHDZ] minutes."

"Spaceheadz minutes?" said Venus. "What are Spaceheadz minutes?"

Jennifer flipped through star charts and planet diagrams on her screens. She called up rows of crazy-looking figures with a wave of one hand. She changed them to Earth numbers with a wave of the other.

"Your Earth days are so sodium-free fast," said Bob.

"But planet [SPHDZ] is very large," said Jennifer. "It takes seven hundred times longer to turn than planet Earth. So one [SPHDZ] hour is seven hundred Earth hours."

"Oh, thank goodness," said Venus. "I like the scientific way this girl thinks!" Venus gave Jennifer a

big hug. "Seven hundred hours divided by twenty-four hours in an Earth day . . .

. . . means we have twenty-nine DAYS to get our one million!"

"Whew," said Michael K., letting go of his stomach.

TJ let out his breath.

"But what was that 'Class Three mess' General Accounting was talking about?" asked Venus.

"Get the code," said Jennifer.

Bob turned the dial on his farm animal See 'n Say to the duck. He pulled the lever. The duck quacked. The

See 'n Say spit out a piece of paper with RED RIDING HOOD printed on it.

Jennifer called up www.imsuregladthatdidnthappen.com on her screen. She entered the code: RED RIDING HOOD.

Venus looked. Venus read. Venus could not believe it. "So that's what would have happened if Michael K. hadn't gotten the blue blob off your shoe?"

"With more flavor," said Bob.

"Wow," said Venus. "That was close, boys and girls."

"Very wow," said Jennifer. "But what are girls?"

Venus looked at Michael K. "You DID tell them about the difference between boys and girls . . . didn't you?"

"Uh, well . . . ," said Michael K.

"Oh, yes," said Bob. "Michael K. told us boys go in the rooms with the sign of 🚹 and MEN."

"Girls go in rooms with the sign of 🚺 and WOMEN," said Jennifer.

"Eeee weee eee ee, eeek ee eek eee ⬛," said Fluffy.

"That's all?" said Venus. "Michael K.!"

Michael K. looked at his shoes. "Okay, so I didn't get into the details yet. Spaceheadz are just made of Energy Waves. They don't need to go to the bathroom! And they don't have anything like boys or girls on their planet."

"This is kind of crazy," said Venus. "But—"

"Hey, wait a minute," said Michael K. "Speaking of crazy, remember when you guys told me that you are thirty-five hundred years old?"

"Oh, yes," said Bob. "Unscented!"

"But that's Earth years?"

"Guaranteed!"

"So if one Spaceheadz hour equals seven hundred Earth hours," said Michael K., "does that mean one Spaceheadz year equals seven hundred Earth years?"

"*NINE OUT OF TEN DOCTORS AGREE*," said Jennifer.

"Then you guys are . . ." Michael K. tried to divide 3,500 by 700 in his head.

"Five years old?"

"One hundred percent," said Jennifer.

Chapter 19

SPACEHEADZ UNPLUGGED

ßпåç´´´åд̃Ω ¨~π¬¨©©´д

ob went back to arranging his bunnies, kitties, ponies, and princesses. He posted his new batch of pictures and checked his friends on his Facebook page.

Jennifer snacked on a handful of Fresh Step kitty litter "with odor-eliminating carbon for maximum odor control." She tuned in to WWE wrestling, clicked on two soap operas, and added more favorite videos to her YouTube channel.

Fluffy hopped on his wheel and spun out a quick Twitter message

> EEE EEEEK SQUEEEK EEEK EEEEKKERS
> SQUEEEEk EEEEP EEEEk SQUEEEEEk.
> EEEE EEEEEEEE EEEKERS. EEEP EEEEE
> EEEEEEEEPPEEEEP.   EEEK !

then typed in "www.fluffysblog.com" on his keyboard to bring up a new blog post. He linked to his newest PowerPoint presentation—"Fluffy for President!"

A whole network of Spaceheadz strangeness suddenly made sense to Michael K.

If he had been in a comic strip, he would have had a lightbulb going on over his head.

"Uh . . . Venus and TJ? Could I talk to you over here for a minute?"

Venus and TJ and Michael K. sat at a beat-up old table along the wall.

"I think I just figured it out," said Michael K. "The Spaceheadz aren't weird just because they are Spaceheadz."

Venus raised an eyebrow. "You mean they aren't weird because they are made of Energy Waves and don't ever have to plug anything in?"

"And watch too many commercials?" said TJ.

"No," said Michael K. "The Spaceheadz are weird because they are five Spaceheadz years old. They are Spaceheadz kindergartners!"

Venus and TJ and

Michael K. watched the three Spaceheadz soaking up TV and computer waves and munching on Fresh Step.

"It would be like following Hugo and Willy to save the world," said Michael K.

"Oh, then this Spaceheadz mission is definitely up to us," said TJ.

"Most definitely up to us," said Michael K.

Mimicry III

You can also get away with a lot by mimicking the look of something bigger and stronger than you.

Moth? Owl?

Owl? Moth?

The Owl Moth:

Meanwhile, back in the bin, Agent Umber could not feel his right arm or his left leg.

"I think my arm and leg have been lasered off by the aliens!" Umber whispered to himself.

They had not.

The heavy boxes of MATH IS COOL! textbooks had just cut off the blood circulation to that right arm and left leg.

The bin suddenly rolled, jolted, wiggled.

Umber heard a truck engine.

The mass of books and boxes shifted above him. They squashed Umber even more.

Umber wiggled his one good monkey-furred arm free. He had to get to his Picklephone®.

Umber stretched.

Umber strained.

He couldn't reach the Picklephone® pocket in his monkey suit.

He was squashed. He was trapped. Tricked by aliens in disguise as a gym teacher and a school nurse, and trapped like a . . . like a . . . like a monkey in a recycling bin.

Umber heard wheels on the roadway, the sounds of traffic.

Where were these fiends taking him? What awful alien plans did they have planned for him? Mind probes? X-ray experiments?

Doughnut making?

Umber realized he could not stand any of those things. If they probed him or x-rayed him or doughnutted him, he would throw up. A lot. He had to escape before they got their hands—or claws or suckers or whatever they really had—on him.

But how?

AAA Kung Fu Plus training, that's how. Take the force greater than you, and redirect it.

Tires squealed. The bin lurched hard to the left.

Umber gathered himself into the *AAA Kung Fu Plus* pose of the growing dragon egg.

The bin swung to the right.

Umber redirected all of the MATH IS COOL! force squashing him and exploded like the DRAGON HATCHING FROM ITS EGG.

"Heeeee-YAH!"

A horn honked. The books shifted!

And then Umber was completely pinned. Now he couldn't move either arm or either leg.

"Maybe I should have tried the DRUNKEN OCTOPUS," Umber muttered into the books now smashing his face.

The truck engine slowed. Umber smelled salt air. He heard seagulls. The aliens were taking him on vacation!

No, wait. Why would they do that? They wouldn't. But they WOULD dump him in the ocean. They were going to dump him in the ocean!

Umber flexed his puny muscles. Now he really wished he had used his Get Huge in Just Three Days! exerciser for more than two days. He could not move.

There was only one thing left to do. Umber didn't want to think about it. But now he had to. It was time to push the Button. The button installed on every AAA agent's phone. The Panic Button.

Umber felt his bin being lowered, then tilted. He could hear waves crashing, metal crunching. He was about to be trash-compacted, pulped, and turned into recycled paper towels.

If only Umber could push his monkey butt against the side of the bin, he could hit the Panic Button and . . . hit the Panic Button and . . .

Umber suddenly realized that he didn't know exactly what it was that happened when you pushed the Panic Button. Something about a signal and a blast? Or maybe a blast and a signal?

The bin tilted up on one side. Umber and the books began to slide to their fate.

No time to think. No time to do anything else. It was time to PANIC!

Umber closed his eyes, jammed his monkey butt against the wall of the bin, and hit the Panic Button.

Right on the button.

Chapter 21

ALBÓNDIGAS

å⌐∫ø˜∂˜☉åß

Dad K. set down a giant, steaming bowl of spaghetti and meatballs on the dinner table.

"My Thursday-night special: **SPAGHETTI ALBÓNDIGAS**! Don't you love the way that sounds? That's Spanish for 'meatball.'"

"We know, Dad," said Michael K. "You tell us that every Thursday when you make **SPAGHETTI ALBÓNDIGAS**."

Dad K. dished heaping plates for Mom K., Michael K., Baby K., and himself.

"Fabulous **ALBÓNDIGAS**. **ALBÓNDIGAS** that's fabulous," said Dad K., trying out new ad slogans like he always did.

"So," said Mom K., "why don't we go around the table and share something new that happened today?"

"Um, right," said Dad K. "Why don't you go first, honey?"

"I'm working on a new project," said Mom K.

"Groo groo, ga gag ahh," said Baby K., putting one handful of spaghetti in her mouth and one handful of spaghetti on her head. She already knew about Mom K.'s ZIA agency and her new project to track unusual patterns in other agencies, such as FEMA, OSHA, and AAA, and to look into ongoing mind-control projects like MK-Ultra, Project Paper Clip, and Project Artichoke.

"My agency is tracking unusual patterns in other agencies."

"Brrrrruup brupp," said Baby K., tracking her meatball with her spoon.

"How about you, sweetie?" said Mom K. to Dad K.

"Oh, gosh," said Dad K., twirling a forkful of spaghetti. "Nothing much, really."

Even Michael K. knew that nothing made Mom K. more suspicious than answering her, "Nothing much." Mom K. suddenly looked very interested in Dad K.'s new project.

"What's it about, darling? Who is it for?"

"Darling" was another dead giveaway that Mom K. was digging for information.

Dad K. didn't notice. "Oh, it's a new slogan campaign. I'm not really supposed to talk about it. Very secret. DarkWave X."

"Brooo?" asked Baby K. She had not heard about this.

Mom K.'s eyebrows shot up. You could almost see her making a mental note.

Michael K. slurped a long spaghetti noodle. Everyone at the dinner table was looking at him. He was next.

"Well," said Mom K. "And what new and exciting thing happened to our big fifth grader today?"

Michael K. took a minute while he was slurping his noodle to think which of the day's new and exciting things he could possibly share.

Baby K. laughed, and tried some more spaghetti on her head.

"Blah grah," said Baby K.

"No kidding," said Michael K.

General Accounting's deadline? That was new. The Spaceheadz' giant blue blob freakout? That was exciting.

"Uh, mostly just regular school stuff," said Michael K.

"Oh, come on," said Mom K. She spotted the BE SPHDZ stickers on his notebooks. "What about your new friends and your Spudz Club?"

"What?" said Michael K. "Oh, you mean the Spaceheadz . . . uh . . . Club. Yeah. Well, I did get some new friends to be Spaceheadz today. But we have to figure out a way to sign up a lot more kids. Quick."

"That is wonderful that you have some new

friends," said Mom K., picking spaghetti out of Baby K.'s hair.

"We have a new deadline. Seven hundred hours to get to a million Spaceheadz. Or the whole planet is a goner."

"Networking. Connecting. Great to make new friends," said Dad K., taking another meatball.

This always happened. Michael K. could tell his mom and dad anything about the Spaceheadz. And they never heard it. Is that what happens to you when you get older? Your brain just can't hear crazy new stuff?

Michael K.'s phone buzzed. A text from Venus. He opened it while Mom K. fussed over Baby K., and Dad K. messed with his meatball.

ROCKING NEW SPHDZ SITE 2NITE.
MEET U 2MORROW A.M. AT SPHDZ HQ B4
SCHOOL.

Another buzz. Text from TJ.

```
MY NEW SPHDZ COMIC IS UP AT
ICKR/TJ/SPHDZ.
ALSO CK OUT: ICKR/TJ/INSECTS
ICKR/TJ/TAGS
```

Michael K. smiled. At least Mom and Dad K. were right about one thing. It did feel good to be connected, networked. It was nice to make friends.

Michael K. texted Venus and TJ back and only half listened as Mom and Dad K. kept talking.

". . . and the strangest sight on my way home from work today . . ."

". . . then our clocks and everything went crazy for a minute . . ."

". . . in a monkey suit, shooting out of a green recycling bin like a rocket!"

"Blagga rum bah," said Baby K.

And, as usual, she was exactly right.

Venus's dad set down a giant, steaming bowl of chicken fried rice on the dinner table.

"My Thursday-night special: **ARROZ FRITO CON POLLO CHANG!**"

"We know, Dad," said Venus. "You tell us that every Thursday when you make chicken fried rice."

"And **FRIJOLES COLORADOS**," said Mr. Chang.

"And red beans," Venus added.

Mr. Chang dished heaping plates for Mrs. Chang, Venus, Hugo, and himself.

Venus picked up her chopsticks and for some reason thought of the new kid, Michael K. How strange was that? That aliens from another planet had come to him? For help saving the world?

"So, what's new at the old schoolhouse?" asked Mr. Chang.

"Oh—I'm making new friends from faraway places, building a new website to save the world," said Venus.

"That's my girl," said Mr. Chang.

"And this morning," said Hugo, "octopuses from outer space attacked the playground." Hugo demonstrated by flopping around like an octopus.

"If it's more than one octopus, you call them octopi," said Mrs. Chang.

Hugo laughed. "Octo pie?"

Hugo flopped his octopus arms again, knocking over his glass of water and his plate of **ARROZ FRITO CON POLLO**.

"Hugo!" said Mr. and Mrs. Chang at exactly the same time.

While everyone jumped up to clean Hugo's mess, Venus used the diversion to hold her phone in her lap.

Mr. and Mrs. Chang did not approve of texting at the dinner table, but they thought it was a great way for Venus to stay connected with friends. A great way to build a network of friends. Right?

Venus sent TJ a text.

Venus sent Michael K. a text.

Mr. and Mrs. Chang cleaned up the last of the Hugo mess and sat down.

Nothing like trying to save the world with

powerful space alien kindergartners. But this could be the scientific discovery of all time. And that Michael K. He was a pretty good discovery too.

Venus smiled and felt good about the Spaceheadz mission. She knew exactly what to do to jazz up the sphdz.com site. She would finish it up and launch it tonight. Starting with changing the name to spaceheadz.com.

Much easier to say.

Much easier to remember.

Because they needed to get going on one million kids remembering—spaceheadz.com.

Vocal Mimicry

Some parrots, blackbirds, and starlings can mimic human speech, music, and random noises.

The greater racket-tailed drongo mimics the songs of other birds.

No one is quite sure why.

Maybe the drongos find more insects by hanging out with the other birds whose songs they mimic.

Maybe the drongos are just messing with the other birds.

The next morning Michael K. skated down Fifth Avenue and met Venus and TJ in front of Spaceheadz HQ. Venus's little brother walked in circles around her. TJ's little brother flapped his arms like

he was flying. Kindergartners. Who can figure out what is going on in their heads?

"Greetings, Spaceheadz," said Venus. "The new site is up and running. We've got an easier sign-up, links to Bob's and Jennifer's and Fluffy's posts, and a spot for millions of kids to send in all their Spaceheadz art and fashion and pictures and ads and videos and everything."

TJ nodded. "It looks good. I linked my Spaceheadz comic. And I spaceheadzed this old deck." TJ held up his skateboard.

"Nice," said Michael K. "Now we are getting somewhere. But how do we get the word out . . . without getting noticed by the AAA?"

Venus spun around, holding on to her little brother's hand. "Well, the first thing I did was change the site name to Spaceheadz.com. You want something people can say. Something they can remember. Then I thought we could meet this morning and do some Spaceheadz brainstorming before school."

The Spaceheadz HQ door opened. Bob, Jennifer, and Fluffy tumbled out onto the sidewalk.

Then Venus and TJ got a real dose of Spaceheadz.

On the short walk to school Bob wandered back and forth on the sidewalk, talking to moms, kids, babies, dogs, and trees.

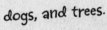

"Lemon-fresh morning, snack-size human," Bob said to a little girl in a stroller. He gave her a **BE SPHDZ** sticker. She smiled and stuck it on her stroller.

"You could have at least taught him to say 'good morning,'" said Venus.

"I tried," said Michael K. "But it doesn't matter. He never remembers. And everyone loves him anyway."

Jennifer walked more carefully, scanning the street like a soldier on patrol.

"And we have got to do something about Jennifer's outfit."

"I think the cleats look kind of cool."

"I want to wear cleats too!" said Hugo.

Venus held Hugo's hand tighter and gave him one of those answers that only a kindergartner would believe.

"You have to be a fifth grader to do that."

"Oh," said Hugo.

They walked by Ralph's TV and Appliance Heaven.

Bob and Jennifer swerved over and pressed their faces against the window to watch *Channel 11 Morning News* on three TVs at once.

"I want to watch TV!" said Hugo.

"I want to watch too," said Willy.

"It's a deodorant commercial," said Venus.

"They are feeding their Energy Waves," explained Michael K. "They have to do something like seven hours of that every day."

"What happens if they don't get their Energy Waves?"

"They get all spazzy and start losing their human shape. Kind of like losing power. It happened once over at my house. We don't want it to happen again."

"I want to feed my Energy Waves," said Hugo.

A man with a briefcase stopped to see what everyone was watching. "Catching up on the morning news? Anything about that giant meteor shower yesterday?"

"*WE RELIEVE PAINFUL ITCHING AND BURNING!*" said Bob.

"*FAST RELIEF,*" said Jennifer.

"*EEEE EEK EEE EEEK,*" added Major Fluffy, hanging out of Bob's backpack.

The man had no idea what to say to this.

"They're not from around here," explained Michael K. "Just visiting. Come on, guys. We better get to school."

"Would you like to be **SPHDZ**?" asked Bob. "***CLINICALLY PROVEN!***"

"***SAFE AND EFFECTIVE!***" added Jennifer.

"Me too!" said Hugo.

"Me too!" said Willy.

"Uh . . . sure," said the man.

Bob slapped a **BE SPHDZ** sticker on his briefcase.

The man smiled and headed off to the subway.

Venus took Hugo's hand and pulled him away from Ralph's TV and Appliance Heaven.

"This is what we have to work with?" asked Venus.

"This is what we have to work with," answered Michael K.

Venus said, "This is like . . . like . . . I don't know what. Like herding cats. Or organizing . . ."

139

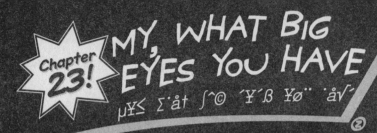
. . . kindergartners.

All eighteen of them. All dressed as Little Red Riding Hood. And all as crazy as . . . kindergartners.

Michael K., dressed in his wolf suit, holding his wolf head under one arm, stood in the middle of the kindergarten classroom.

A tornado of kindergarten chaos swirled all around him.

Little Red Kristen was crying because the bow on her cape wouldn't stay tied. Little Red Hugo and Little Red Willy crawled on the floor howling, pretending to be wolves chasing Bunny Bob and three more bunny imitators. A whole pile of Little Reds banged on the pots in the kitchen corner, dancing with Jennifer and two more Little Reds who decided they wanted to wear granny wigs too.

Michael K. remembered why he didn't like to be the group leader of anything.

"You are the Big Buddies group leader," Miss Singer had said.

"Just run them through the play practice like we did yesterday," Miss Singer had said.

"I have to run down to the office for five minutes," Miss Singer had said.

That was probably just two minutes ago, but it seemed like two years ago.

"Okay, Red Riding Hoods," said Michael K. in his most teacherly voice. "Let's get into our groups for play practice."

The wolves kept howling.

The bunnies kept hopping.

The grannies kept dancing.

Friendly Woodsman TJ tried to catch a few wolves and slow them down. They escaped by crashing through the block corner.

Red's Mom Venus tried to corral some stray hopping bunnies. They slipped under the sand table.

"Michael K.!" said Venus. "You are the group leader. DO SOMETHING!"

Michael K. wasn't quite sure what to do. What would Miss Singer do? She would clap her hands. Then everyone would listen.

Michael K. clapped his hands.

A couple kindergartners stopped. Then Jennifer and her grannies banged their kitchen-corner pots. And everyone went nuts again.

Or what about that song? What was that song Miss Singer used? Michael K. couldn't remember.

Now the wolves were chasing the grannies. Now the bunnie

were chasing the wolves. Little Red Kristen cried louder.

A song. Any kindergarten song.

Michael K. did not usually sing songs. But Michael K. was desperate. Michael K. started singing the first song that popped into his head:

"IF YOU'RE HAPPY AND YOU KNOW IT, CLAP YOUR HANDS!"

Clap, clap.

"IF YOU'RE HAPPY AND YOU KNOW IT, CLAP YOUR HANDS!"

Hugo and Willy stood up and clapped their hands.

Clap, clap.

"IF YOU'RE HAPPY AND YOU KNOW IT . . ."

The bunnies and grannies stood up and joined in.

". . . AND YOU REALLY WANT TO SHOW IT, IF YOU'RE HAPPY AND YOU KNOW IT, CLAP YOUR HANDS!"

The whole class joined in.

Clap, clap.

Venus tied Little Red Kristen's bow and smiled at Michael K.

TJ gave Michael K. a thumbs-up and joined in the next verse.

"IF YOU'RE HAPPY AND YOU KNOW IT, TOUCH YOUR NOSE. IF YOU'RE HAPPY AND YOU KNOW IT, TOUCH

YOUR NOSE. IF YOU'RE HAPPY AND YOU KNOW IT, AND YOU REALLY WANT TO SHOW IT, IF YOU'RE HAPPY AND YOU KNOW IT, TOUCH YOUR NOSE."

One minute later, when Miss Singer walked back in the classroom door, she saw an amazing sight.

She saw eighteen Little Red Riding Hoods sitting in a circle quietly listening to the Wolf.

Chapter 24!
UMBER UNDERGROUND
¨μ∫´® ¨~∂´®◎®ø¨~∂

The morning traffic on the Brooklyn-Queens Expressway thundered overhead.

"Like a herd of elephants," said Umber.

Umber adjusted the orange cones around the manhole cover, fixed the AAA Sewer Cleaning sign, zipped up his green plastic AAA Sewer Cleaning coveralls, and climbed down the metal ladder into the old sewer pipe.

His whole body ached from getting squashed in the recycling bin yesterday.

And he still smelled like burned monkey fur.

Umber clicked on his AAA HelmetLite/HelmetCam® and saw he was standing in a small stream of brownish green water.

Okay. Change that label on the map from **UNUSED SEWER MAIN** to **SLIGHTLY USED SEWER MAIN**.

So yes, he had pressed the Panic Button. Now he knew what it did. It did that POP thing with the flare and that *bang whoosh* thing with the rocket. Ouch.

But . . . he had escaped the awful aliens.

And here he was, right back in the fight.

Agent Umber of the AAA would not let a little thing like a squashed arm and a squashed leg and a slightly burned butt keep him from protecting and serving and always looking up!

Well, okay. Right now he was technically looking down, and into some murky smelly darkness . . . but he was protecting! And serving! And bringing in those aliens with a brilliant new Agent Umber Plan—sneaking into a *secret pipe* entrance!

Something splashed in the darkness ahead.

Umber raised his AAA HelmetLite/HelmetCam®.

Cement, slime, and water.

Umber lowered his AAA HelmetLite/HelmetCam® to check his map.

Left . . . right . . . left . . . right . . . right.

"Right," said Umber, narrating for his HelmetCam®. "Right under P.S. 858 is where that will put me. And won't a certain nurse and a certain gym teacher be surprised to see me?"

Umber crouched over and slogged through the sludge. The pipe was just big enough for Umber to bend over and duck-walk through. The small beam of light from his AAA HelmetLite/HelmetCam® bounced off the slimy inside curve of the pipe and a trickle of gunk running down the center.

Trucks and cars rumbled overhead.

Umber continued his narration. "Agent Umber pushes bravely into the dark sliminess. Very dark. Very slimy. A strong smell. Whew. A bit like old cheese, dirty socks, and . . . urgh—Brussels sprouts."

Umber did not like Brussels sprouts.

Umber slipped on the curved sides of the pipe, soaking first one shoe, then the other.

Umber swore, "Ah, Brussels sprouts!"

Maybe this wasn't such a smart plan, he thought. What if I get lost? What if I get stuck down here forever? What if a giant blind rat and a huge white alligator attack me at the same time and rip my arms and chew my legs and . . .

"Aaaaaah!" Umber screamed.

The scream echoed down miles of wet and dark and smelly underground pipe. No one heard it. (Well, no one except one small rat flipping somersaults in midair like a sewer trapeze artist.)

Umber's mom always said he had a "vivid imagination."

Sometimes he scared himself.

Umber stopped shuffling and took a deep breath. That didn't help much. The deep breath tasted like cheese-covered Brussels sprouts. With a side order of old socks.

Umber tilted his head back. The AAA HelmetLite/

HelmetCam® beam lit up a metal plate bolted to the inside of another pipe running straight up.

"Bingo," said Agent Umber. "This must be it. Look out, aliens, here comes Umber!"

Agent Umber climbed up the metal rungs inside the rising pipe.

He flashed his light on the metal plate to read the raised letters.

And just as he read aloud the words "P.S. 858 Waste Line Overflow," he heard a distant rumble . . . and what sounded like the splash and rush of water.

The good news about working on the kindergarten play was that the fifth graders got to go to early lunch.

The bad news was that lunch was so not worth getting to early.

Michael K., Venus, TJ, Bob, and Jennifer sat with their lunch trays at the far corner table.

"Why is the dog hot?" said Bob. "And do we really have to eat him?" Bob pulled out his notebook and showed Michael K. his page of cute puppy pictures.

Jennifer took a bite of fish burger. She quickly spit it out on the table and smashed it flat with her fist. "Yuck. Bad." She pulled out a handful of smelly markers and nibbled the end of a Wild Cherry Red. "Mmmm. Good."

"That was pretty amazing," said Venus.

"Like magic," said TJ, sketching a picture of Michael K. in his wolf suit, taming a crowd of wild kindergartners.

"How did you do that?" said Venus.

Michael K. rolled his Tater Tots around on his lunch tray. "It was easy," he said. "Just like what my dad does at his advertising company every day. It's a jingle. Songs stick in people's heads. People remember slogans and jingles."

"FROSTED LUCKY CHARMS . . . THEY'RE MAGICALLY DELICIOUS," sang Venus.

"MR. CLEAN CLEANS YOUR WHOLE HOUSE, AND EVERYTHING THAT'S IN IT," sang TJ.

Bob added, **"SNAP! CRACKLE! POP! RICE KRISPIES!"**

"MY BOLOGNA HAS A FIRST NAME, IT'S O-S-C-A-R," sang Jennifer.

Fluffy poked his head out of Bob's backpack. He sang/squeaked, **"MEOW MEOW MEOW MEOW, MEOW MEOW MEOW MEOW, MEOW MEOW MEOW MEOW MEOW MEOW MEOW."**

Venus gave Fluffy a funny look.

"Exactly," said Michael K. "And the jingle actually makes people do what the advertisers want—they remember the name of the product, and they go out and buy it."

Bob sang, **"THE BEST PART OF WAKING UP . . ."**

Michael K. continued. "Did you know that the first singing commercial was on the radio? In 1926. It was for Wheaties. And after people heard the jingle, they went out and bought fifty thousand cases of Wheaties in just one town."

"That's crazy," said TJ.

Jennifer sang, *"RICE-A-RONI . . . THE SAN FRANCISCO TREAT."*

"Hey, that's it!" said Michael K.

Venus lifted up her fish burger bun to get a closer look at the actual fish burger. It did not look good. "What's it? We should be eating Rice-A-Roni?"

"No," said Michael K. excitedly. "This is the answer to our Spaceheadz problem. This is how we spread the Spaceheadz word. We need a Spaceheadz jingle!"

Venus thought about this. Venus slapped the bun back down on her fish burger.

"That is a great idea," said Venus. "But what are we going to use for a Spaceheadz jingle?"

Venus and TJ and Michael K. spent the rest of the lunch period trying to come up with a good jingle. Nothing quite worked, but Michael K. felt that TJ and Venus really got what he was talking about. Michael K. felt something good.

But some of the other early lunch students

felt something else. They felt their stomachs rumbling. They felt their fish burgers and hot dogs fighting their way back up.

Because before the school year started, P.S. 858 had gotten a great deal on some old U.S. Army fish burger and hot dog meals. There was no expiration date on the boxes. But there was a drawing on one of the boxes:

This drawing was famous during World War II. Right around 1944 or so.

A fresh fish burger and hot dog meal is pretty bad. But an old fish burger and hot dog meal is very bad.

The first wave of early lunchers started running for the bathrooms and losing their lunches. They were quickly followed by everyone else (except Jennifer and Bob and Fluffy, who had not taken even one bite).

The toilets were soon flushing overtime.

Which was why the P.S. 858 main waste line was soon filled up.

Which was why a tidal wave overflow of fish burger chunks, half-chewed hot dog bits, and plenty more you don't want to know about roared into the P.S. 858 Waste Line Overflow.

bathrooms

Chapter 26!

BLEEEEAAAUUUGH!
∫¬´´´åå姴·····©´/

A gent Umber looked up to shine his AA HelmetLite/HelmetCam® into the darkness and s what was making that rushing sound

So the first wave of PS. 85 waste overflow hit Umber fu in the face and knocked hin

down into the main pipe.

The rest of Umber's ride was captured, in full brown-and-green detail, by the waterproof (and gunkproof) AAA HelmetLite/HelmetCam®.

The swell of half-digested fish burger, partially chewed hot dogs, soggy buns, and toilet water pushed Agent Umber facedown along the slimy outlet pipe. He

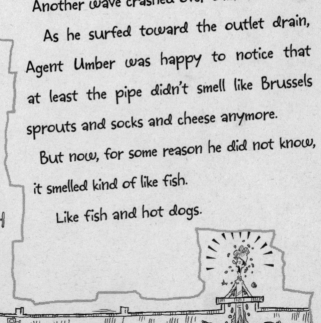

finally got his hands out in front of him to stop his tumbling. Now he was bodysurfing the rolling wave of flushed stuff.

Umber surfed and slipped and slid.

He wasn't sure what had caused this sudden overflow, but he thought it would probably be a good idea to try to keep his mouth shut.

Another wave crashed over Umber's head.

As he surfed toward the outlet drain, Agent Umber was happy to notice that at least the pipe didn't smell like Brussels sprouts and socks and cheese anymore.

But now, for some reason he did not know, it smelled kind of like fish.

Like fish and hot dogs.

Like really old fish and really old hot dogs.

Umber surfaced and took a big gulp of air . . . and also, unfortunately for him, a big gulp of some chunky bits and yellowish green water.

Umber's last bit of narration for the AAA HelmetLite/HelmetCam®?

"Bleeeeaaauuuugh!"

"R emember to check our class website's homework page," said Mrs. Halley, "www dot Mrs. Halley's comets dot com. Reading assignments, spelling words, your reports on your Big Buddies projects. And please come to watch your classmates tonight in their Little Buddies' 'Little Red Riding Hood' play."

A small brown dog sat on the curb outside P.S. 858, waiting.

Mrs. Halley's Comets grabbed their books and bags and backpacks. They streamed out the door of room 501-B, down the stairs, through the door, and out to the sidewalk.

"I've got a bad feeling about tonight," said Michael K.

"It's probably just leftover bad-fish-burger feeling," said TJ.

"I'm sure that AAA agent is still on our trail. What if he tries to bust the Spaceheadz tonight? At the play?"

"How can we stop him?" said Venus. "Do we even know where he is?"

The small brown dog trotted up to the group of Bob, Jennifer, Michael K., Venus, and TJ. He pointed his nose toward Bob's backpack and barked, "Arf, arf."

Fluffy popped his head out.

"Eeek?"

"Arf, arf, arf. Woof woof woof woof."

"Eee EEE!"

"Woof woof yap yap yap. Arf arf. Bark bark, arf arf arf. Yipe! Woof woof woof. Grrrrrrrr . . . rarf rarf rarf?" asked the dog.

"Oh, boy," said Michael K. to Venus and TJ. "There is one other thing I should probably tell you."

Fluffy smoothed his whiskers. He answered.

"Arf arf . . . arf yipe yap arf. Bark bark, woof woof. Woof yipe yap bark.

"Owoooooo rarf woof. Woof woof woof. Bark yap yap yap yap yap yap. Yip yip. Woof woof. Bark bark bark bark, bark-bark. Bark woof woof arf arf arf arf. Yowooooo! Yip yip bark woof, woof bark yip bark. Arf arf-arf-arf. Bark woof-woof bark arf arf arf. Arf bark woof-woof bark arf arf."

The dog replied. "Arf
woof. Woof woof woof.

"Bark yap yap woof yap. Yip yip. Woof woof. Bark bark bark bark, bark-bark. Bark woof woof arf arf arf arf. Yip yip bark woof, woof bark yip bark. Arf arf-arf-arf. Bark arf arf arf. Arf bark woof-woof bark arf arf.

"Woof woof. Yap yap bark bark bark. Bark bark bark bark, bark bark bark woof. Woof woof woof woof, woof woof woof. Bark yap yap yap yap yap yap. Yip yip. Woof woof. Bark bark bark bark, bark-bark. Bark woof woof arf arf. Yipe arf arf woof. Bark woof woof yip yip grrrrrrrrrrrrrrrr.

"Slobber slobber, sniff sniff sniff sniff.

"Woof woof. Yap yap bark bark bark. Bark bark bark bark, bark bark bark woof. Woof woof woof woof, woof woof yip woof bark woof. Woof woof woof. Bark yap yap yap yap rarf yap yap. Yip yip. Woof woof. Bark bark bark bark, bark-bark-bark. Bark woof woof arf arf. Yipe arf arf woof. Bark woof woof yap.

"Arf woof. Woof woof woof. Bark yap yap

woof yap. Yip yip. Woof woof. Bark bark bark bark, bark-bark. Bark woof woof arf arf arf arf. Yip yip bark woof, woof bark yip bark. Arf arf-arf-arf. Bark arf arf arf. Arf bark woof-woof bark arf arf.

"Woof woof. Yap yap bark bark bark. Bark bark bark bark, bark bark bark woof. Woof woof woof woof, woof woof woof. Bark yap yap yap yap yap yap. Yip yip. Woof woof. Bark bark bark bark, bark-bark. Bark woof woof arf arf. Yipe arf arf woof. Bark woof woof yip yip grrrrrrrrrrrrrrrr.

"Slobber slobber, sniff sniff sniff sniff.

"Woof woof. Yap yap bark bark bark. Bark bark bark bark, bark bark bark woof. Woof woof woof woof, woof woof yip woof bark woof. Woof woof woof. Bark yap yap yap yap rarf yap yap. Yip yip. Woof woof. Bark bark bark bark, bark-bark-bark. Bark woof woof arf arf. Yipe arf arf woof. Bark woof woof yap."

"Woof woof woof," said Fluffy. "Bark yap yap

yap yap yap yap. Yip yip. Woof woof. Bark bark bark bark, bark-bark. Arf woof. Woof woof woof. Bark yap yap woof yap. Yip yip. Woof woof. Bark bark bark bark, bark-bark. Bark woof woof arf arf arf arf. Yip yip bark woof, woof bark yip bark. Arf arf-arf-arf. Bark arf arf arf. Arf bark woof-woof bark arf arf.

"Woof woof. Yap yap bark bark bark. Bark bark bark bark, bark bark bark woof. Woof woof woof woof, woof woof woof. Bark yap yap yap yap yap yap. Yip yip. Woof woof. Bark bark bark bark, bark-bark. Bark woof woof arf arf. Yipe arf arf woof. Bark woof woof yip yip.

"Arf woof. Woof woof woof. Bark yap yap woof yap. Yip yip. Woof woof. Bark bark bark

bark, bark-bark. Bark woof woof arf arf arf arf. Yip yip bark woof, woof bark yip bark. Arf arf-arf-arf. Bark arf arf arf. Arf bark woof-woof bark arf arf.

"Woof woof. Yap yap bark bark bark. Bark bark bark bark, bark bark bark woof. Woof woof woof woof, woof woof woof. Bark yap yap yap yap yap yap. Yip yip. Woof woof. Bark bark bark bark, bark-bark.

"Woof woof. Yap yap bark bark bark. Bark bark bark bark, bark bark bark woof. Woof woof woof woof, woof woof yip woof bark woof. Woof woof woof. Bark yap yap yap yap rarf yap yap. Yip yip. Woof woof. Bark bark bark bark, bark-bark-bark. Bark woof woof arf arf. Yipe arf arf woof. Bark woof woof yap.

"Woof woof. Yap yap bark bark bark. Bark bark bark bark, bark bark bark woof. Woof woof woof woof, woof woof yip woof bark woof. Woof woof woof. Bark yap yap yap yap rarf yap yap. Yip yip. Woof woof. Bark bark bark bark, bark-bark-bark. Bark woof woof arf arf. Yipe arf arf woof. Bark woof woof yap. Bark woof woof arf arf arf arf. Yip yip bark woof, woof bark yip bark. Arf arf-arf-arf. Bark woof-woof bark arf arf arf. Arf bark woof-woof bark arf arf?"

The dog scratched behind his ear. Then he answered.

"Yap yap bark bark bark. Bark bark bark bark, bark bark bark woof. Woof woof woof woof, woof woof woof bark woof. Woof woof woof. Bark yap yap yap yap yap yap. Yip yip. Woof woof. Bark bark bark bark, bark-bark. Bark woof woof arf arf. Yipe arf arf woof. Bark woof woof.

"Yip yip. Woof woof. Bark bark bark bark, bark-bark. Bark woof woof arf arf. Yipe arf arf woof. Bark woof woof yip."

"Rowf!" said Fluffy.

"Arf arf," said the dog.

And he trotted off.

Venus and TJ looked at Michael K.

"Huh?" said TJ.

"Whaaaa . . . ?" said Venus.

Bob translated for Fluffy.

"The AAA man tried to get into P.S. 858 through under-the-ground pipes."

"Really?" said Venus. "And we know this because that dog just told . . . a hamster?!"

"One hundred percent," said Bob.

"That's the other thing I was going to tell you," said Michael K. "Fluffy knows a lot of different languages."

"The man got flushed out," said Bob. "The dog heard it from his friend the rat."

"Oh," said Venus, still looking completely shocked. "It'd be helpful to have a Fluffy translator."

"Eek ee," said Fluffy.

"He says he's working on it," translated Bob. "He's putting it on his blog."

DUCK, DUCK ...
DARKWAVE X

Chapter 30!

$\partial\ddot{\varsigma}° \leq \partial\ddot{\varsigma}° \geq \geq \geq \partial\mathring{a}®°\Sigma\mathring{a}\sqrt{}´ \approx$

I. TWELVE GEESE
12:30 P.M.

Afternoon quiet in Greenwood Cemetery. Quieter than usual.

The geese had found the small pond in the northwest corner.

They had plenty of water, and no magnetic reason to go anywhere.

II. THE AD FACTORY NY
12:30 P.M.

Dad K. leaned over his authentic factory workbench. The nicked and scarred surface was piled with papers covered in Dad K.'s notes and scribbles.

Brand manager Brad stuck his head in the doorway. "Lunchtime, Special K!"

"Oh, hey, Brad," said Dad K., covering his paper with one arm. "No lunch for me today. I have to get this . . . uh . . . thing out right away."

"What thing is that?"

"Um, nothing," said Dad K., stacking up his papers and shoving them in the black folder with the red X.

Brad turned his head to try to read the folder. "Whatever you say, Mr. K." Then Brad was gone.

Dad K. typed the last of his slogans into a text document, trying each one out as he typed.

1. Got what?

2. For good. For you.

3. What would you do with _____?

4. Say yes to _____!

5. Aren't you glad you _____?

6. SNAP! CRACKLE! _____!

Dad K. took one more look over his work, then sent it to DarkWave X's blind e-mail address like he was instructed.

He gathered up the black folder and hid it in the back of his file cabinet. He didn't realize he was still talking to himself.

"What the heck? Good slogans and jingles don't just fall out of the air. How do they expect a good slogan for something I don't even—"

"Ping!" went Dad K.'s e-mail in-box.

The e-mail sender address was a single X.

Who was that? They couldn't have read it all that fast. Could they?

There was no doubt whom it was from. The single line read: *Very good. Await further instructions.*

III. HAIR TODAY/ZIA
12:30 P.M.

"Hello, Chrissy. Afternoon, Carol," Mom K. called to the Hair Today stylists at the shampooing sink and the hair dryers.

Chrissy nodded.

Carol nodded.

Mom K. took her seat in the last chair and spun silently

into the secret ZIA offices . . . with her afternoon coffee break Diet Coke.

In her office she pushed aside the stack of top-clearance-only research folders on her desk to make a little room. A narrow piece of paper fell out of the folder marked MIND CONTROL.

And Mom K. probably wouldn't even have noticed it, but something about the logo caught her eye.

Mom K. took a swig of Diet Coke and read the company name: DarkWave X.

She put down her Diet Coke and read on.

IV. SUNNY SUN SUNSHINE DAY CARE, BROOKLYN
12:30 P.M.

Baby K. sat up in her crib, eyes half closed, chubby knees bent, bottoms of both feet touching, tiny hands folded in her lap.

A fly buzzed in front of the window in a never-ending figure eight.

Baby K. tasted the buzzing sound.

Baby K. smelled the pale blue color of the sky.

Baby K. heard the lingering taste of her afternoon apple juice on her tongue.

Baby K. felt the thick odor of burning leaves.

Baby K. heard the warmth of the afternoon sun on her leg.

Something big was growing.

Baby K. couldn't tell what it was just yet.

But, sitting there perfectly balanced for the moment, she knew it with all of her senses.

The chief sat in his swivel chair, bent, twisted to one side, hunched over, peering over his latest measurements.

Bah. This would not do.

He needed more.

This was his chance to take care of unfinished business.

This was his chance to make the universe right.

Vocal Mimicry II

Whales change their songs by mimicking parts of other whale songs.

After park rangers moved an orphaned African elephant to a national park near a busy highway, they started hearing trucks rumbling down the highway . . . when there weren't any trucks.

It was the elephant.

She was mimicking the truck sounds.

Doesn't it make you wonder what the ants might be up to?

Later that evening the light of the full moon, 245,314 miles away, reflected down on the sign on P.S. 858: PARENT-STUDENT-TEACHER NIGHT!

Behind the curtain onstage, Michael K. peeked out at the audience.

Michael K. had never seen such a frightening sight. The cafeteria-gym-auditorium was packed with parents and teachers and kids.

Mrs. Halley was in the center. Mr. Booley, the computer teacher, stood back by the coffee and doughnuts. Mom, Dad, and Baby K.—third row, on the right. Venus's and TJ's parents behind them. Nurse Dominique and Mr. Rizzuto right in the front row.

Michael K. dropped the curtain shut. He started sweating. It might just have been the fuzzy wolf suit. But he was mad nervous, too.

Bunny Bob showed Little Red Hugo his one-footed bunny hop. Granny Jennifer showed Little Red Willy her newest wrestling move—a jumping high kick. Venus adjusted her Little Red Riding Hood's Mom dress. Woodsman TJ added some color to the side of his cardboard ax.

Little Red Madison stepped on Michael K.'s wolf tail. Again.

How could this NOT go wrong?

What if someone brought blueberry yogurt? Or blueberry pudding? Or blue Jell-O?

Michael K. imagined the Spaceheadz tornado of folding metal chairs that would be triggered. With the parents and teachers still in them.

Not good.

And what did that AAA agent know? Was he onto them? Would he make a move tonight?

Michael K. peeked out again to scan the audience and look for the AAA agent. That fat guy with the mustache? The skinny one with the black suit? The lady in the pink and green swirly dress? He could be disguised as any one of them.

This was not good, not good, not good.

Michael K. picked up his tail and padded over to Mom Venus and Woodsman TJ. "Guys, this is not good. We have to get the Spaceheadz out of here. We are going to get busted for sure."

"Don't be such a worrywart," said Mom Venus. "No one can even tell who we are in these costumes."

"Except our moms," said Woodsman TJ.

"Though I still can't believe you got us stuck doing this," said Mom Venus. "And I can't believe

you 'forgot' to tell us about a talking hamster."

"No kidding," said TJ.

The lights in the cafeteria-gym-auditorium dimmed.

A microphone squealed and someone coughed into it.

"I know," said Michael K. "This whole play mess is my fault. But let's get out while we still can. We have to save the world, right? We can say we got sick."

"All of us at one time?" said Venus.

"Bad fish burgers?" said TJ.

A spotlight lit a small circle in the center of the curtain.

Miss Singer clapped her hands softly three times. "Places, children."

Principal Edison started talking. His amplified voice bounced off the back wall, up over the rafters, down through the heavy red velvet curtain. It reached the Red Riding Hood actors sounding like: "Bwaa bwa bwa, bwumf fuff fuuf. Ruhr ruhr ruh ruh ruh. Mumph

murr murrr, muhr muum muum muuum."

Miss Singer herded the whole class of wandering Red Riding Hoods next to Mom Venus for the opening scene.

"Bwa bwaa, bwa murf maay mwa-mwa. Mihm mihm: mming mu muhmer mih muh!"

The curtains swung back.

Bright white lights blinded the Red Riding Hoods, their Mom, their Granny, the Bunny, the Woodsman, and the Wolf.

So none of them saw the giant doughnut slip in the back door.

The first part of the play went off as smoothly as a play full of eighteen kindergartners all dressed exactly alike possibly could.

The Reds were told to take the basket of goodies to Granny. They skipped through the woods. They saw Bunny Bob. They met the Wolf. The Reds sang while the Wolf beat them to Granny's house and stuffed Granny in the closet.

Then the second part of the play started.

"My, what big ears you have," said the flock of Little Red kindergartners.

"The better to hear you with," said

Wolf Michael K., the sound of his own voice booming inside the big wolf head.

"My, what big eyes you have," said the Red Riding Hood chorus.

"The better to see you with," said Wolf Michael K.

The piano played a little introduction. All of the Red Riding Hoods shuffled into a line facing the audience and sang their "Little Red Riding Hood" song.

"HEY THERE, LITTLE RED RIDING HOOD.
YOU SURE ARE LOOKING GOOD.
WATCH OUT FOR THAT BIG, BAD WOLF
    FROM THE WOODS.
OWOOOOOOOO!"

The red-hooded Little Buddies sang their hearts out. Mostly.

Well, not really.

About half of them forgot all of the words. Little Red Madison looked for her mom. Little Red Benjamin picked his nose. Little Red Katie watched the nose-picking Little Red Benjamin.

But the parents and teachers didn't seem to notice.

They clapped like it was the best thing they had ever seen.

The Little Red Riding Hoods smiled.

Wolf Michael K. was just starting to feel like they might get through this whole play night without a problem . . . when he saw something that didn't look right.

Michael K. saw something large at the edge of the audience. Something strange. Something moving toward the stage.

Still in Granny's bed, disguised as Granny, Wolf Michael K. tried to sit up and get a better look through his small wolf-head eyeholes.

He saw Nurse Dominique and Mr. Rizzuto still right in front.

He saw Mom, Dad, and Baby K. still off to one side.

And then, toward the back, near the coffee machine,

he saw a sight that chilled him even in the sweaty heat of his furry wolf suit.

Michael K. saw a giant doughnut.

More exactly—a man in a giant doughnut suit. It was the same man Michael K. had once seen in a giant taco suit.

It was Agent Umber from the AAA.

THE SOUND OF ONE DOUGHNUT CLAPPING

Chapter 33!

†´´ ßø¨˜∂ øf ø˜´ ∂ø¨©´˜¨† ç¬å∏∏ˆ˜©

Ⓩ

Agent Umber, agent of many disguises,
slipped in the back door of the P.S. 858
cafeteria-gym-auditorium just as the curtain
was rising.

No one noticed the giant doughnut standing by the coffee and doughnuts.

Just like Agent Wild Blue Yonder had sug-
gested. It was the perfect disguise. Hiding in
plain sight.

Umber scanned the crowd. He was on the inside now. He knew they were probably here somewhere. He looked for telltale signs of aliens and alien activity.

The stage lights flashed different colors. Could be Alien Energy Wave movement. The metal school bell on the wall looked dented. Definite alien interference.

But maybe the aliens had changed shape.

Maybe they weren't disguised as the nurse and the gym teacher anymore.

Umber scanned the kids onstage.

Bunch of Red Riding Hoods. One of the Red Riding Hoods looking for her mom. One of the Red Riding Hoods picking his nose. One of the Red Riding Hoods watching the Red Riding Hood picking his nose. Nothing.

Wolf, Granny, Bunny, Woodsman.

Was that Wolf looking at him? No. Nothing.

Umber tried to pour himself a cup of coffee. But his doughnut arms were too far apart. Umber forgot about the coffee.

More songs. More dancing. Terrible.

Half the kids didn't even know the words.

"Concentrate, Umber," said Agent Umber. "Don't be such a loser!"

Which kind of annoyed the little old lady next to him. Umber hadn't realized he'd said anything out loud.

"Didn't realize I'd said anything out loud," said Umber to the little old lady.

This annoyed her even more.

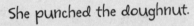

She punched the doughnut.

Umber moved along the wall, closer to the stage.

Umber was worried. Not so much about the punch. Though it did kind of hurt. But about the aliens. No sign of aliens. Another dead end? A bust? Another disgrace in his file?

Umber swept the crowd with his agent vision. He was just beginning to panic . . . when he spotted exactly what he was looking for.

White blouse, white skirt, white shoes.

The same blue and white Yankees jacket he had seen from his recycling bin hiding place.

Side by side.

It was them!

Doughnut Umber edged closer to the stage. He bumped parents and teachers with his glazed sides. But he didn't care. His AAA agent heart was racing. This was it. The real deal. He was on the case!

Umber positioned himself carefully. He would make quick, quiet work of this alien arrest. He would wait for the right moment, then swoop in quickly and quietly. Like a doughnut in the dark.

The kid dressed as a wolf onstage finally said something about his big teeth.

The piano played.

Then all heck broke loose onstage—singing, dancing, all those kids running around in one big red circle. The perfect cover. This was the right moment.

"Protect and serve, and always look up!" cried the doughnut as he charged the alien school nurse and gym teacher.

But it's too bad he didn't look down.

He might have seen the little old

lady's foot sticking out in the aisle.

Umber tripped. Umber fell. Umber missed his alien target and rolled onstage, a giant doughnut in the spotlight.

**EXACTLY THREE
MINUTES EARLIER . . .**

The Red Riding Hoods finished their song.

The parents and teachers clapped and cheered.

Michael K. danced his way over to Mom Venus and Woodsman TJ, stage right.

"What are you doing?" whispered Venus. "It's not the Wolf and Woodsman dance yet."

"It's Agent Umber!" Michael K. wiggled his wolf head around, trying to make it look like part of the show. "In the audience. The giant doughnut."

Mom Venus looked out and spotted the dough-nut. He was kind of obvious. Kind of hard to miss. "Oh, no. We are totally caught now. What do we do?"

Wolf Michael K. thought for a second. Then he decided to at least go down fighting, trying to save the world. "TJ, you grab Bob. Venus, get Jennifer. Make a run for it. I'll take out the doughnut."

"I don't know," said Venus.

"We have to do it," said Wolf Michael K. "If the AAA catches the Spaceheadz, it's lights-out for all of us."

Venus looked into the Wolf's eyeholes.

"Okay," said Venus.

The Wolf, Red's Mom, and the Woodsman danced their way across the stage.

Miss Singer played the scary intro notes of the next song.

TJ tried to get Bob to hop off the stage. Bunny Bob did not want to.

Venus tried to get Jennifer to leave her closet. Granny Jennifer did not want to.

Michael K. faced the doughnut approaching the stage.

Miss Singer played the scary intro notes of the song again. She nodded her head at Michael K.

"My, what big TEETH you have," said Miss Singer.

"My, what big TEETH you have," repeated most of the Little Red Riding Hoods.

Doughnut Umber edged closer.

The spotlight shone on Michael K., center stage. It was his line. He had to say it.

"The better to . . . EAT YOU WITH!" roared Wolf Michael K.

The piano broke into the frantic music for the Wolf-chases-Red scene.

Just like in play practice, Wolf Michael K. chased the flock of Red Riding Hoods in one big circle.

Not at all like in play practice, the doughnut charged and came rolling across the stage.

Wolf Michael K. chomped his big teeth and waved his big claws to save the Spaceheadz, but there were just too many Red Riding Hoods in the way.

Wolf Michael K. went down. Through his

wolf-head eyeholes all he could see was a swirl of little red riding capes and little dancing feet.

Wolf Michael K. groaned. He had failed. He had let down his friends. He had missed the doughnut, lost his Spaceheadz pals, and very probably turned off his entire planet.

He howled a sad howl and collapsed in a small wolf heap.

FINALE

f^~å¬´

W hat Michael K. didn't see was the doughnut roll . . . and roll and roll and roll.
The doughnut rolled from stage front to stage
back, rolled right down the back steps, rolled out
into the alley, and rolled smack against the side
of the empty recycling bin that had just been
returned there yesterday.

A third grader in the audience asked his mom, "Is there a giant doughnut in the Red Riding Hood fairy tale?"

"I guess there is in this one, sweetie," said the mom.

Nurse Dominique and Mr. Rizzuto got up and went out back to check on the dazed doughnut.

The kindergarten Red Riding Hoods, still stunned by the sight of a giant doughnut rolling through their play, stopped dead in their tracks. They forgot to sing. They forgot to dance. They forgot to act.

There was a pause.

And then things really got weird.

Bunny Bob knew what to do. He knew what always happened next after the action paused. Bunny Bob hopped to the center of the stage and announced in a clear, loud, very unbunnylike voice, "And now a word from our sponsors."

Granny Jennifer popped out of the closet with a rolled-up tube of paper under her Granny-nightgowned arm.

"Runny nose? Sore throat? Aches and pains?" said Granny Jennifer.

The parents and teachers in the audience gave a nervous little laugh.

Miss Singer, at the piano, actually opened her mouth in surprise.

Wolf Michael K. couldn't make sense of what he was hearing. Was that Bob? Was that Jennifer? Where was the AAA doughnut? Wolf Michael K. struggled to get out from under the three Little Red kindergartners still sitting on his back.

Little Red Willy and Little Red Hugo wandered up to center stage to see what their Big Buddies pals were doing. Bunny Bob and Granny Jennifer were now holding the big roll of brown paper between them.

Together they said, "You need strong relief! You need to . . ."

They unrolled the paper between them to show a gigantic stenciled logo, which they then shouted:

Little Red Hugo and Little Red Willy cheered and clapped for the Spaceheadz commercial.

The rest of the Little Red kindergartners cheered and clapped and went kindergarten crazy. Bunny, Granny, and eighteen Little Reds twirled around the stage.

M iss Singer looked stunned.

The audience looked like Miss Singer.

Michael K. struggled to his feet. He looked around in a daze. No doughnut anywhere. Spaceheadz-inspired kindergarten chaos everywhere. If he didn't do something, the Spaceheadz were in trouble for sure. Michael K. knew what he had to do.

Michael K. ran to center stage and sang, "IF YOU'RE HAPPY AND YOU KNOW IT, CLAP YOUR HANDS!"

Clap, clap.

The song worked its magic instantly.

A couple of the Little Reds joined in.

"IF YOU'RE HAPPY AND YOU KNOW IT, CLAP YOUR HANDS!"

Clap, clap.

Bob, Jennifer, and the rest of the Little Reds joined in.

Miss Singer had no idea what had happened to the play, but she saw the song was calming the craziness, so she played along on the piano.

"IF YOU'RE HAPPY AND YOU KNOW IT, AND YOU REALLY WANT TO SHOW IT, IF YOU'RE HAPPY AND YOU KNOW IT, CLAP YOUR HANDS!"

Clap, clap.

The audience looked relieved.

Miss Singer looked relieved.

Then Bob and Jennifer (and Fluffy sticking out of the pocket of Bob's Bunny suit) took everyone to a whole new level.

Bob sang: "IF YOU'RE SPHDZ AND YOU KNOW IT,

CLAP YOUR HANDS!"

Clap, clap.

And of course the kindergartners joined in.

"IF YOU'RE SPACEHEADZ AND YOU KNOW IT,
CLAP YOUR HANDS!"

Clap, clap.

Now half of the audience joined in.

"IF YOU'RE SPACEHEADZ AND YOU KNOW IT,
AND YOU REALLY WANT TO SHOW IT . . ."

The rest of the audience joined in.

"IF YOU'RE SPACEHEADZ AND YOU KNOW IT, CLAP YOUR HANDS!"

Clap, clap.

The P.S. 858 parent-student-teacher group clapped their hands, stomped their feet, and waved their arms.

All to show that they were Spaceheadz.

And they knew it.

Mom Venus and Woodsman TJ stood next to Wolf Michael K., watching the crazy scene.

Venus recorded one more verse on her phone.

The audience stood up, clapping and cheering.

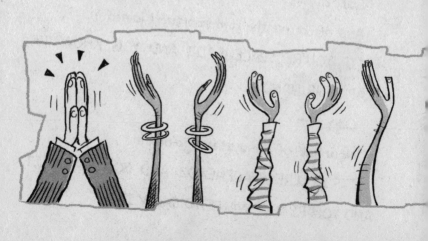

The Little Red Riding Hoods bowed.

"I think we have our Spaceheadz jingle," said Wolf Michael K.

"This is going up on the site tonight," said Venus.

The three fifth graders watched the crowd going nuts.

"Hey," said TJ. "What ever happened to that AAA doughnut?"

"Good night, sweetie."

"Good night, Mom," said Michael K.

"You were a very good wolf tonight."

"Thanks, Mom."

"Kind of different 'Red Riding Hood' than the one I knew when I was a kid," said Dad K. "I don't remember the whole doughnut and clap-your-hands parts of the story."

Mom K. and Dad K. stood in the doorway of Michael K.'s bedroom.

"That was something new," said Michael K., propped up in bed, clicking on the new spaceheadz.com website. He saw that Venus had already posted the video. "That was something new and a little spaceheadz."

"I think it's wonderful that you are making so many new friends," said Mom K.

Michael K. looked at the Spaceheadz counter. It was clicking steadily up as he watched.

"Thousands of them," said Michael K.

Vocal Mimicry III

"Oh, be quiet."

"Oh, be quiet."

"You are a doofus!"

"You are a doofus!"

"I know you are, but what am I?"

"I know you are, but what am I?"

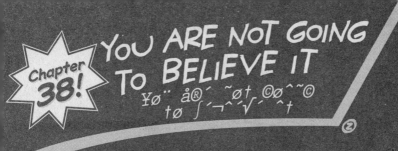
T he early-morning sun barely warmed the crisp fall air.

Michael K. was not used to seeing early-Saturday-morning sun. He preferred early-Saturday-morning sleep. Or early-Saturday-morning cartoons. Or early-Saturday-morning just-messing-around.

But Venus had something she wanted them all to see. And there was no saying no to a determined Venus.

"You are not going to believe it," said Venus. She grabbed Michael K. and pretty much pulled him all the way down to Fourth Avenue. A sleepy TJ rolled on his Spaceheadz skateboard. Bob and Jennifer ran behind.

217

They stopped at a construction site next to Sergeant Sanders's Alabama Fried Chicken place.

Venus pointed to the plywood boards surrounding the site.

The boards along Fourth Avenue were covered by one giant drawing.

"Did you do this?" asked Venus.

"No," said Michael K.

"Well, I didn't do it. TJ didn't do it. And Bob and Jennifer didn't do it," said Venus.

"Eee eek," said Fluffy, out of Bob's pocket.

"And Fluffy didn't do it," said Bob.

"So do you know what that means?" asked Venus.

Michael K. was still a little fuzzy from last night's play and being pulled out of bed way too early.

"We are buying advertising?"

"No!" said Venus. "It means our Spaceheadz jingle is working! Someone else did this. The Spaceheadz word is spreading all over the Web and beyond."

Michael K. looked at the giant Spaceheadz tag again.

It looked very cool.

Venus flipped open her phone. "Look at this. Space-headz stickers in Chicago. Spaceheadzed ads in Florida.

Someone painted a Spaceheadz mural in San Francisco.
This guy spaceheadzed his skate shoes in Texas. Space
headz drawings in China!"

"No way," said Michael K.

But then he looked at the pictures, and there they were.

Spaceheadz everywhere.

"But I saved the best for last," said Venus. She punched
up a website and handed the phone to Michael K.

It was their new spaceheadz.com site.

Michael K. looked at the Spaceheadz counter. Then he
had to look again.

"Four hundred ninety-seven thousand eight hundred and
ninety-one?" said Michael K. "That's almost half a million."

"And most of that is overnight!" said Venus.

"Clinically proven **SPHDZ**," said Bob.

"Safe and effective **SPHDZ**," said Jennifer.

Someone leaned out a passing car and yelled, "BE SPACEHEAAAAAAADDDDDZZZZZ!"

"Fast-acting, new and improved Spaceheadz," said Michael K.

A giant Bunny Bob hopped happily around the table.

Fluffy waved his arms in time to music that only he could hear.

Granny Jennifer cranked the egg-beater and punched the green button on her George Foreman grill.

The microwave hummed and transmitted this message:

MISSION SPACEHEADZ
FROM: SPHDZ
TO: GENERAL ACCOUNTING
BRAINWAVE NUMBER NOW 500,002 AND
COUNTING.
REPORT:
IF YOU ARE SPACEHEADZ AND YOU KNOW IT,
CLAP YOUR UPPER BODY PARTS TOGETHER!
IF YOU ARE SPACEHEADZ AND YOU KNOW IT,
CLAP YOUR UPPER BODY PARTS TOGETHER!
IF YOU ARE SPACEHEADZ AND YOU KNOW IT,
AND YOU REALLY WANT TO SHOW IT,
IF YOU ARE SPACEHEADZ AND YOU KNOW IT,
CLAP YOUR UPPER BODY PARTS TOGETHER!
SETTING: DEFROST
POWER: FULL
TIME: 1:20

END

Two blocks down from the BE SPHDZ construction site billboard, under the same weak Saturday-morning sun, a lone doughnut walked slowly home.

Cars zoomed by him on the avenue. His van had been towed. Again. Of course.

And that was not the worst of it.

The doughnut held two tickets. One a summons for impersonating a doughnut, and one a summons for disrupting a school event.

The doughnut was still trying to piece

together exactly what had happened, exactly what had gone so wrong last night.

He had been so sure. But the last thing he remembered about the alien-bust-gone-wrong was rolling across that stage, rolling down some stairs—and then there they were, hovering over him, ready to tear him apart and turn him into alien goo.

Umber had been ready to take them in the hard way. But there had been just one small problem.

The school nurse and the gym teacher were not aliens.

Though the nurse was a former Brooklyn detective, 78th Precinct. Which did explain how she knew that very painful arm-twist lock.

Umber stretched his still-sore doughnut arm.

They were both totally human. Too bad it had taken all night for the 78th Precinct detectives to make sure Umber was totally AAA.

Any agent could have made the same mistake.

Well, probably not Agent Hot Magenta.

Could this be any worse?

It could.

Umber's Picklephone® buzzed.

He couldn't have answered it if he wanted to. Because of the whole doughnut arm thing. But he didn't want to. Didn't need to. He knew who it was. And what he would say.

The Picklephone® buzzed.

A giant eighteen-wheel Dunkin' Donuts semi-truck thundered past.

The driver honked.

The doughnut sighed.

Two rings, three rings, four rings.

"You have reached the secret message machine of . . . *AGENT UMBER* . . . Please leave your coded message at the beep." *BEEEEP.*

The chief closed his sleek spider phone. He didn't have to leave a message. His call would be enough. Umber would think he was in trouble.

The chief looked over his AAA HQ monitors.
The squirrels were back in their
trees in the park.

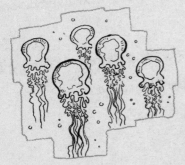

The jellyfish were back
floating calmly in the aquarium.

The elephants were back
napping in the zoo.

Ants, bees, rats, and fleas were back doing what ants, bees, rats, and fleas do.

The black and orange butterfly, definitely a bitter-tasting monarch, launched from its perch and flapped its wings.

Twelve geese took off from Greenwood Cemetery.

They followed a wave, a current of energy, a magnetic path not visible to the human eye.

They formed a perfect V.

The chief smiled in the half darkness of HQ Central Command.

Umber had messed up again.

Umber had messed up . . . perfectly.

Saving the world continues in SPHDZ Book #3!

JON SCIESZKA'S

ILLUSTRATED BY SHANE PRIGMORE!

Spaceheadz

Book #3!

WITH SUPER HAMSTER GRIP!

SPHDZ

HO, HO, HO!

Two small elves stood in line behind the red ropes outside Dunker's Donuts on Fifth Avenue in Brooklyn.

This was not as completely crazy as it might sound, because there was also a sign in the Dunker's Donuts window that read:

The two elves stood in line with the rest of the moms and dads and babies and kids waiting to tell Santa what they really wanted. The two elves wore those green elf outfits you've seen in cartoons and movies and cookie commercials.

But the strange thing about these two elves was that one of them wore soccer cleats and the other one wore a SpongeBob SquarePants backpack . . . that was carrying another tiny, hamster-size elf.

"What are you going to ask Santa to bring you, Chelsea?" the mom in front of the elves asked her daughter.

"A pony," said Chelsea, kicking her little brother.

"Oooooh," said the SpongeBob-backpack elf. "More flavor! I'm going to add a pony to our list."

"We are already asking Santa for one hundred more SPHDZ," said soccer-cleats elf. "Can he also fit two ponies in his flying-sled delivery system?"

"Eeek squeak squeak eeek," said hamster elf. "Squeee week wee eek."

"Great whole-grain jingle bells!" said soccer-cleats elf. "This Santa Claus is super-size and great taste!"

"Eee eee eee eeek?" asked hamster elf.

"Yes," said backpack elf. "That is a most extra-crunchy idea. I will send a visual image of us to Michael K. and Venus."

"Ho, ho, ho," said the suspiciously skinny-looking Santa in the Holidayz HoHoHoles Korner of the Dunker's Donuts. "I don't think Santa will be able to get you a real F-18 Hornet fighter jet."

The little boy in Santa's lap punched Santa in his red velvet stomach and pulled Santa's white beard down under his chin. "You are a stupid Santa."

The backpack elf held a camera out at arm's length.

"Squeeek," said the hamster elf.

The elves twisted their faces into something like smiles.

The hamster elf nodded.

The camera took a picture.

"Come on, Jackson," said the little boy's mom. "We will go talk to Santa's manager about this."

The dad took Jackson's hand and glared at Santa. "I can't believe I had to buy a dozen Holidayz HoHoHoles for this. All you had to do was say 'Okay.'"

"I could look into procurement of the F-18," said Santa, replacing his beard and fixing his stomach. "But I am pretty sure it is not in line with federal procedure to release these fighter jets to citizens."

The dad stared at Santa.

"There would also be a lot of paperwork. But maybe the older model F-111 might be available?"

Now both the mom and the dad were staring at Santa.

Santa realized he had almost for-
gotten to say the required Dunker's
Holiday Saying. He added, "Ho, ho, ho.
Dunker's knows what dunkers love."

The mom and dad and punching kid
stormed over to talk to the manager.

The line and the elves moved three
steps closer to Santa.

Hamster elf sent off the picture
and text.

"Eeee eee, eee eee."

**CLINICALLY PROVEN SAFE AND
EFFECTIVE**," added backpack elf.
"Michael K. and Venus are going to be
sooooo surprised!"

SHHHHHHHHHH!

Michael K. and Venus sat at the table farthest away from the librarian.

Venus flipped open her sparkly and -stickered laptop and logged on to the library's free wireless.

"Check this out," whispered Venus.

Venus launched spaceheadz.com and quickly clicked

SPACEHEADZ IN ACTION

"Spaceheadz drawings from Magic BBQ Sauce in Seattle, Washington . . .

"Spaceheadz ads from Toll-Free Fusilli in Lebanon, Indiana . . .

"Spaceheadz music from All-Natural Oven Cleaner in Toronto, Ontario . . .

"Spaceheadz stories from Bold Taste Deodorant in London, England . . .

"Spaceheadz videos from

Disposable Chicken Fingers in Barcelona, Spain . . .

"We really did it, Michael K.," whispered Venus. "We really connected a whole Spaceheadz network."

"Wow," said Michael K.

He had been so busy going to school, spreading the Spaceheadz word, and trying to keep Bob and Jennifer and Major Fluffy out of trouble . . . that he hadn't stopped to look at the whole thing. It was pretty amazing.

"And coolest of all . . . ," whispered Venus. She clicked back to the Spaceheadz home page and zoomed in on the counter. "We are almost at our three point one four million plus one Spaceheadz to save the world."

Michael K. read the Spaceheadz counter aloud, "Three million one hundred thirty-nine thousand nine hundred and one Spaceheadz? WOO!"

The librarian, at the other end of the room, gave Michael K. a stern look.

Michael K. ducked his head.

"This is great. This is huge. I can't believe we are going to do it," whispered Michael K. "Only one hundred more Spaceheadz to go. This is amazing."

Michael K. stared at the spaceheadz.com counter. Then he had another thought.

"But what if something goes wrong?"

Venus clicked through more Spaceheadz drawings and Spaceheadz ads. "You are such a downer sometimes. We haven't seen the AAA in weeks. And Bob, Jennifer, and Major Fluffy have been almost normal. What could go wrong?"

"I don't know," said Michael K. "You know how weird stuff just seems to happen with Spaceheadz."

Venus ignored Michael K. She clicked happily through more Spaceheadz pages. "SPHDZ *DOES IT BETTER!*'

'I'M A SPHDZ / YOU'RE A SPHDZ / WOULDN'T YOU LIKE TO BE A SPHDZ TOO?' 'MAKE FRIENDS WITH SPHDZ, MAKE SPHDZ WITH FRIENDS!' Space-headz kids are geniuses!

"And check this out," said Venus. "Our three point one four million plus one moment is going to be historic. I'm recording the final counter moments in the Spaceheadz admin section so we can have them forever."

Venus clicked on the tiny words SPHDZ ADMIN at the bottom right corner of the spaceheadz.com page, right next to TERMS OF USE and PRIVACY POLICY. It opened a page asking for another password. Venus typed VENUS. The secret recording page popped onscreen. "Cool, huh?"

"Yeah," said Michael K., trying to ignore the feeling in his gut. "That is cool. What could go wrong?"

Michael K.'s phone and Venus's phone buzzed with incoming texts at exactly the same time.

Michael K. checked the sender.

MAJOR FLUFFY

Michael K. opened the message. It read:

EEEEK EEE EEE EEEE EEEK.

Michael used "Fluffy's Translator" to translate the message into English.

MORE FLAVOR! DELICIOUS IDEA.
ASKING NOW OF SANTA FOR MORE SPHDZ!

This message made Michael K. a bit nervous.
Michael K. looked at the picture.

This made him completely freaked out.

"AHHHHHGGGG!" croaked Michael K., pointing at the picture.

"WHAT?" said Venus.

"EEE ARRR GAHHH UHHH!"

Michael K. was so spazzed out that he could not manage to say any real words. He pointed at the face over elf Bob's shoulder.

"That's cute," said Venus. "The Space-headz are visiting Santa."

Michael K. zoomed in on the face revealed by the pulled-down Santa beard.

Michael K. regained just enough power of speech to yell four words.

"Not Santa! Agent Umber!"

The librarian got up from her desk to remove the noisemakers from the quiet room.

But Michael K. and Venus were already out the door, running like the future of the world depended on it.

And it did.

ABOUT THE AUTHOR
AND ILLUSTRATOR

JON SCIESZKA has recently been named the first National Ambassador for Young People's Literature by the Library of Congress. He is the author of some of the best known and funniest books written for children, including *The True Story of the Three Little Pigs*, the Time Warp Trio series, and the Caldecott Honor Book *The Stinky Cheese Man and Other Fairly Stupid Tales*. *Smash! Crash!*, his most recent picture book, was on the *New York Times* bestseller list for several weeks. He is a former elementary school teacher and an avid promoter of literacy—particularly for boys. His website guysread.com focuses on his national campaign. Jon lives with his family in Brooklyn, New York.

SHANE PRIGMORE is currently a development and story artist at Dreamworks Feature Animation. He was a principal character designer on the stop-motion feature *Coraline*. Shane lives in California.

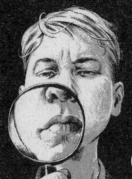